THE ISLAND HIDEAWAY

Getaway Bay, Book 3

ELANA JOHNSON

ISBN-13: 978-1638760054

Chapter One

Z ara Reddy pulled her dark hair out of its ponytail, the amount of water squeezing out with her elastic making a huge puddle on the floor. She was used to being wet, because she worked as a synchronized swimmer on the island on Getaway Bay, in some of their most popular shows.

This summer's show kept her busy with practices during the week, and nightly shows from Thursday to Sunday. She didn't work the matinees, thankfully. She was grateful for the jobs that always seemed to come her way. That way, she didn't have to go to work at her family's Indian restaurant in downtown Getaway Bay.

They were traditional in every sense of the word, and Zara had made more explanations about her life choices over the years than she cared to admit.

Her phone flashed violently with blue and green

lights, and she checked her texts first as the other swimmers came into the locker room.

"Are you coming with us to dinner?" Suzie asked, taking Zara's attention from her device.

"Oh, uh, I don't think so," she said, lifting her phone. "I think I just got that house-sitting job."

Suzie wrung out her hair and started changing. "That's great, Zee. Up on the bluffs?"

"Yeah. First time." She was an experienced house sitter, and she'd completed a dozen or so jobs now. It was easy work, and she got to stay in some of the nicest houses on the island.

And this one?

This one was the crown jewel of the mansions up on the bluff. She'd been texting back and forth with a woman named Petra for several days now, and Zara had never answered so many questions. It was house sitting, not rocket science.

But Petra wanted a background check, and Zara's references, and if there would be any pets in the house. Zara did have a long-haired white cat, but she'd kept that to herself. Petra didn't seem like the kind that would tolerate felines.

The pay was sky high, and Zara smiled as she tapped out her acceptance of the job. She had a small apartment in a long row of them, and staying up on the bluffs would add to her gasoline bill, but it would be so much better than listening to the thirty-somethings next door try to become Hawaii's next big boy band—at all hours of the night.

The address to the house appeared on her screen, along with the code to the gate and the garage. *Anytime tonight or tomorrow,* Petra said. *Send me your PayMe, and I'll get you the money.*

Zara showered and dressed, throwing her heavy bag full of suits, props, caps, nose clips, goggles, and more over her shoulder and heading out to her car. Hopefully, it would start. It was much too hot to sit in the car without air conditioning, listening to the engine click while she prayed it would turn over.

"With this new job," she muttered to herself as she crossed the parking lot. "You can maybe afford to buy a new car." One that actually started the first time.

Sighing, she got behind the wheel and stuck in the key. Miraculously, the car started with the first turn, and she fiddled with the dials on the air conditioner to make it blow harder. Her phone rang, and she answered the call from one of her best friends, Ash Fox.

"Hey, Ash." Zara put the car in reverse, trying not to let any of the jealousy she'd been experiencing when it came to Ash infuse her voice. See, Ash had been Zara's go-to friend when everyone else had a boyfriend. Ash never did. Ash sat behind her sewing machine almost all the time. Zara could always count on Ash—until Burke.

And now Zara had a huge, empty house on the bluffs to go home to.

"So remember how you said you might be able to help out at Your Tidal Forever?" Ash asked.

"Yeah," Zara said slowly.

"Well, Hope is *swamped*, and she's looking to pick up a few seasonal people this summer. Just until the Bellagio wedding is over in September."

Normally, Zara would've jumped at the chance, because it was work, and she didn't pass up an opportunity to make connections around the island in case she met someone who could open another door for her.

Anything was better than the door leading to Indian Room.

"I can't," she said, infusing the appropriate amount of disappointment into her voice. "I just picked up that house-sitting job I was telling you about. With the show, and now this, I'm not sure I'll have time."

"Oh, that's fine," Ash said. "Hope just said to spread the word. If you know anyone, have them call over to Your Tidal Forever and ask for her assistant, Shannon."

"I will." Zara knew Shannon too, and how she worked so closely with Hope and didn't go insane was a quiet miracle.

"So you got the house-sitting job?" Ash asked.

"Yes." Zara smiled as she turned onto the road that led back to her apartment. She just needed to pack a few things and get Whitewater, her cat, into her carrier. "I'm pretty excited about it. I'm heading up there right now."

"Pool?" Ash asked.

"*Big* pool," Zara said. "In fact, I think there are two pools at this place."

"I have four dresses to make by next weekend." Ash moaned.

"I'll be here until September," she said. "In fact, I think I'm going to give up my lease." After all, it was only June, and she could save three and a half months of rent if she gave up her place. There were plenty of rentals on the island, and she wouldn't have any problem getting somewhere else come fall.

Not only that, but then the boy band wannabes wouldn't be her neighbors anymore. Oh, yes, she was going to give up her apartment, just as soon as she made it back down to town from the bluffs the following morning.

Tonight, she was going to bask in the grandeur of this mansion, maybe sit by the pool, and just *relax*.

AN HOUR LATER, THE SUN WAS NOWHERE NEAR SETTING, for which Zara was thankful. She didn't want to pull up to the house in the dark, but Whitewater would not get in her carrier and it had taken Zara an extraordinarily long time to pack a bag and leave her house with the cat. The backs of Zara's hands could testify of that, what with all the scratches from Whitewater's protests.

The cat yowled from the passenger seat, and Zara said, "Oh, be quiet, Whitey. You're fine." So maybe the words held a bit of exasperation. But some of those scratches were deep, and two had bled a little. So the cat could be quiet as Zara navigated the twisty road up to the bluffs.

All of Getaway Bay's rich and famous lived up here. Okay, fine, not all of them. But all the ones who didn't live in the swanky penthouses on the beach. Beachside didn't exist up on the bluffs. Oh, no. People bought these houses for the privacy and security, as well as the stunning, spectacular, three hundred and sixty degree ocean views.

Zara couldn't decide which she'd rather have. Soft, white sand right out her back door, or a mansion in the hills. But for the next three months, she'd be taking this twenty-minute drive up to the mansion.

She turned onto the appointed road and went about a block before she met a closed and locked gate. After keying in the code, her excitement grew while the gate rumbled open. A sprawling piece of land sat before her, and she eased her car through the now-open gate onto the driveway.

With the gate moving closed behind her, another sigh passed through her body. She had tomorrow off from swimming practice, as the director was working with the acrobats and the main characters in Fresh Start, the not-to-be-missed show of the summer in Getaway Bay's outdoor theater pool.

Zara had done a few shows at the same venue, and the special effects capabilities were superb. She'd also worked with Ian Granger, the director, several times, and while she'd thought they might have a spark in the beginning, it had fizzled fast.

Just like every other relationship Zara had had. She'd been in the dating pool for a long time, and she was feeling wrinkly and dried out from all the chemicals. She wouldn't care that much that she was boyfriend-less if her mother didn't badger her constantly to find that special someone.

As if Zara hadn't been looking.

She gazed at the beautiful Hawaiian flowers, the trees, the black lava rock in the landscaping. This was done by a professional, and Zara loved every piece of it as she drove slowly past.

The house sat down a little hill and it too spread out and up, boasting tall white pillars on the front porch, which faced the ocean. Of course, three sides of this house faced the ocean, and Zara hoped the room where she'd be staying had a walk-out balcony. Or a patio. Something where she could step from inside to out and breathe in the fresh air and hear the waves crashing on the rocks far below.

She pulled up to the front door and peered through the windshield. "All right, Whitey," she said to the cat. "Let's go see where we're going to be living for a few months."

Petra never had to know about the cat. The woman said she and her family would be overseas for the summer, thus the need for a house sitter. So Zara killed the engine, walked around the car and shouldered her overnight bag before picking up the cat carrier.

At the front door, she keyed in the code and the lock disengaged. The alarm sounded once, and she stepped over to the keypad to disarm it. She hadn't gotten a separate code for it, so she put in the same numbers she'd used to unlock the front door.

But that only made the alarm beep at her. The steady, every-two-second beeps made her want to stab something in her ears. She tried the code again, very aware of Whitewater's increased yowling. It was as if the cat was trying to harmonize with the incessant beeping.

"Come on," she muttered when she put in the wrong digit and had to go back.

She became aware of another sound amidst the chaos—growling. She turned to see a big, black dog standing about ten feet away, his teeth bared.

"Oh," Zara exhaled most of the word as Whitewater started hissing inside the carrier. The dog barked, huge, booming sounds that filled the two-story high foyer.

With the beeping, and the hissing, and the barking, it was a miracle that Zara heard someone say, "Boomer, be quiet," just before a man came through the doorway and stood behind the dog. He paused when he caught sight of Zara, his eyes widening. He lifted the spatula he held like he'd use it to defend himself if necessary.

"What are you doing here?" he yelled over the barking, the hissing, and the beeping.

"House-sitting," she yelled back. "Who are you?"

He looked like he could be a fashion magazine model, what with that dark hair all swept back into a man-bun on the back of his skull. He opened his mouth, presumably to yell something else, and then rolled his eyes before striding forward.

"I changed the code," he said, practically pushing her aside to punch in the numbers. The beeping stopped. He turned back to the dog. "Boomer, quiet." The dog stopped barking, and Zara tried not to be impressed.

Tried, and failed.

"Sit," the man said next, and the dog did that too.

Now, if she could get Whitewater to stop hissing....

Their eyes met, and dang if Zara didn't have to jump back at the shock she received. He had gorgeous eyes the color of the black lava rock outside, and his olive skin had certainly been featured in many a woman's daydreams about European beaus.

"Who are you again?" she asked, realizing he'd never said.

"I'm Noah Wales," he said. "And I don't need a house sitter."

Chapter Two

Noah Wales would not be swayed by a beautiful pair of eyes. Or all that dark skin. Or the curves this woman possessed. Oh, no. He would not.

Wasn't that the whole reason he'd come to the island house in the first place? To get away from women like the one standing in front of him?

Yes, yes it was.

He blinked and backed up a step, though this was his house—fine, his family's house—and he didn't have to go anywhere. He gripped the spatula he'd been using to flip eggs, wondering why he still held it.

She blinked too, confusion coloring those dark, chocolatey eyes. He hated that description, as if everything had to be related to food. But when he tried to come up with another way to categorize her eyes, it was related to coffee.

He sighed. "Did my mother hire you?"

"Is your mother named Petra?"

"Yes," he said. "But you said it wrong. It's not Petra, like your cat is a pet. It's Petra, like...peat moss."

"Petra," she said correctly, swinging the cat carrier behind her back as if Noah hadn't already seen it. "Then, yes. Your mother hired me."

Noah's mind raced. He didn't want his mother to know he was here. He didn't want *anyone* to know he was here. He didn't want this woman here with him. He just needed somewhere to lie low for a while until he could figure things out, repair his reputation, and then return home to Triguard.

"What's your name?" he asked.

"Zara Reddy." She extended her hand like they'd be bunkmates. He looked at it for a moment past comfortable and then gave it one pump.

Could he send her away? Would she text his mother?

Her phone shrilled out a few quick beeps in a row, stealing her attention and giving him some time to think. She tapped out a quick response and looked at him. "So, what are we going to do?"

"Well, I really don't need a house sitter," he said. Boomer's claws clicked against the tile as he came closer. "As you can see, I have a guard dog. So I'll be fine."

"I need this job," Zara said, her phone chiming in rapid succession again. "I've already sent your mom my payment info."

Noah nodded. "That's fine. She doesn't need to know." So maybe he spoke the last sentence with a little too much feigned nonchalance, because Zara's perfectly sculpted eyebrows went up.

"She doesn't?" She cocked her hip and put the hand holding her phone on it. "Does she even know you're here?"

"This is *my* house," he said. He didn't have to defend himself to her. An inward sigh practically had him giving up. The truth was, he had to defend himself and his actions to everyone. He had since the moment he was born into the royal family, the Wales of Triguard.

"Your mother hired me this afternoon," Zara said, a definite measure of desperation in her words.

"I'll bet she said no pets." He cocked an eyebrow at the cat carrier, where a definite low meow still emanated.

"You have a dog," she said. "And he's huge, and he's definitely the shedding type."

"This is my house," he repeated, wondering if she'd even heard him the first time.

Her phone rang this time, and she sighed like he was the most annoying man on the planet, and said, "Excuse me a moment, would you?" She lifted her phone to her ear without waiting for him to say anything. "Hey." She turned her back on him and wandered a few steps further into the house.

Noah needed to get rid of her. If any reporters saw her come through the gate, there'd be a dozen cameras watching the place. Where had she parked? Probably right out in the open, and he groaned as he turned to look out the tall, skinny windows that flanked the front door.

Yep, her beat-up sedan sat right there, out in the open for anyone to see.

"Sorry," she said, and he turned back to her. "There's this huge celebrity wedding on the island this fall, and the owner of the wedding planning place needs extra hands all summer." She shook her head as if she was saying something crazy, but Noah seized onto the information.

"Is she paying or is it volunteer work?" If he could get some volunteer credit, maybe he could start to repair some of the damage he'd caused in Venice....

"I think she's paying." Zara squinted at him. "Why?"

"Why what? Nothing."

"You have a look in your eye."

"What look?" He scoffed. "You met me five minutes ago. I don't have a look."

"Mm hm," she said, nodding. "I know your type. Rich, spoiled, handsome. Living up here on the bluffs like you own the world just because you can see a lot of it. Always looking to play an angle. What is it this time? Knocked up a woman and need to play nice with the press now? Or maybe...maybe you've had a bit of a scandal and need a way to clean up your image."

Noah simply stared at her. Had she crawled inside his mind and rooted around in there until she'd found his exact situation?

"I have not knocked anyone up," he said with disgust.

"And I really can't have the press here. So I need you to move your car. Now." Had she said he was handsome?

Yeah, right after rich and spoiled.

"Where?" she asked.

"The garage," he said. "Then we'll talk some more about...stuff."

"Stuff?" She stood there with that strap over her shoulder, her bag bumping her hip.

"An arrangement," he said, the idea swirling around in his mind. "I'll go put coffee on. Unless you prefer tea?"

She blinked at him, and Noah himself was a little weirded out by the way he was whiplashing between polite and defensive.

"Coffee's fine," he said, moving away from her. As he went, he caught the scent of her perfume, and it was part flowers and part something else that he couldn't quite name. As he left her in the foyer and entered the kitchen, the word came to mind.

Chlorine.

She smelled like chlorine. He checked over his shoulder to make sure she hadn't followed him, and relief ran through him when he heard the front door open and close. "All right," he said to himself and Boomer as he filled the coffee pot with water. "Let's just hear what she has to say, okay? Maybe this won't be so bad."

Zara took so long to return to the house that Noah thought she may have left. But she'd left her bag and her cat in the front foyer, so he poured himself a cup of coffee and waited. After all, he was the youngest child of a king, and waiting was practically part of his genes.

When she finally did come in, it wasn't through the front door but the one that led into the garage. "This place is huge," she said. "Did you know there are four doors leading out of the garage? I thought I'd never find my way inside."

Noah smiled at her, enjoying the exuberance in her expression. "Well, you found the right one at last." He indicated the coffee pot and the ruby red mug he'd gotten down for her. "Coffee?"

She eyed him as she moved closer and poured her own cup of coffee. After putting in a spoonful of sugar and quite a lot of cream, she stirred and faced him again. "So, Noah. You sounded like you had a plan."

"Sort of," he said, his mind still tripping on some of the finer details. "Where did my mother say you'd be sleeping?"

Zara set her coffee mug on the counter and pulled out her phone. "Let's see. She said I could have any of the guest rooms to the right of the main staircase, or I could stay on the main level in any of the three rooms on the west side." She looked at him. "I thought you didn't need a house sitter."

"I don't."

"Then what—?"

"I need the privacy of this place," he said carefully. "I know my parents won't be back for months. I need to… lie low for a while. No one can know I'm here." He didn't know Zara at all, but she seemed like a smart woman. Her quick wit while they'd traded jabs in the foyer told him she might be able to pick up what he was laying down without him having to spell it all out.

"So you want me to 'house sit.'" She made air quotes around the last two words. "To keep people away? So they think no one's here?"

"Bingo," he said. "And you can stay here. Get paid for sitting the house. Lie by the pool. Bring up groceries. Whatever you were planning on doing."

"Bring up groceries," she said. "You mean *your* groceries."

"I might make a few requests," he said as if that were a perfectly reasonable thing for him to do. Then he wouldn't have to go into town. The idea really was coming together. "Everyone will think the house is empty. The paparazzi and cameras won't need to stay or try to find me here."

"Whoa. Paparazzi?"

"They're relentless," he said. "And they know I left Venice." He hoped they didn't know where he'd gone yet. He really just needed some time.

"Oh, of course," Zara said with sarcasm dripping from the words. "Venice."

Noah regarded her coolly. So she was beautiful. Smart. But she had a cat, and he generally disliked felines. Boomer didn't seem to mind, as he'd followed Noah back into the kitchen and now lay panting near the fridge.

"So here's my deal," he said. "You can stay here as you'd planned. Pick any of the rooms on my mother's list, but I am staying on the second floor to the right of the staircase. Use the pools. All of that." He took a step toward her, surprised and even more attracted to her when she didn't back away from him.

"But no one can come up here. So no pool parties or anything like that. You'll get the groceries and other things I might need so I don't have to leave the house. You'll still get your summer here. You'll get paid."

"And you? What do you get from this?" She folded her arms. "Because I'm not one of *those women*." Her dark eyes flashed dangerously.

Noah laughed. "Trust me, Zara. I'm not one of *those men* either. I just got out of a really bad relationship. I'm not looking for another one."

"Or a summer fling," she said. "I don't do flings."

"Great. Makes two of us." Just because she made his stomach flip didn't mean he was going to act on the attraction.

"You still haven't said what you're getting from all of this," she said. "Except me buying your groceries and running your errands and taking care of *your* house."

Perhaps she had heard him when he'd said this place was his.

"I get the time I need," he said. "The anonymity I've never had. And the chance to volunteer on that celebrity wedding."

Her eyebrows went up again, and he wondered if she

practiced such a flawless motion in the mirror. "Why would you want to do that?" she asked.

"I have my reasons," he said. He'd been raised to serve others, and volunteer work *was* the best way to repair bad public perception. Now, if Noah hadn't been "the bad boy of Triguard," he definitely wouldn't have logged over ten thousand volunteer hours over the past thirty-one years of his life.

"So what do you think?" he asked, calmly taking another sip of his coffee, the way he'd seen his father do many times.

Zara studied him for several long moments, clearly working through something in her mind. Probably a lot of somethings. Finally, she said, "I think I'm crazy. I can't believe I'm going to say yes to this."

Noah grinned at her and plucked his own phone out of his shorts pocket. "Great. I'm just going to need the number of that wedding planning place...."

Chapter Three

Zara stood in the doorway of Bedroom Number Three, deciding it was the best one. It sat way down at the end of the hall, past the other two rooms. It had its own attached bathroom, and it had a set of double doors directly ahead where the evening sunlight still shone through.

She groaned as she stepped across the threshold, her overnight bag holding hardly anything but weighing so much on her shoulder. Probably because she'd been carrying it for the past twenty minutes as she figured "stuff" out with Noah.

"You must be insane," she muttered to herself as she closed the door behind her. The knob had a lock, which she pressed, and then she could truly relax. Not that she thought Noah would come barging into her bedroom. For some reason, she got the vibe that he'd stay up on the second floor this summer. Even the pool was too out in the open for him, something she'd gathered as the panic from having her car parked by the front door instead of in the garage had rolled across his face.

And yes, there were four doors leading out of the garage, but Zara wasn't an idiot. She'd just needed some time to do a little Google-Fu online. Noah Wales was a prince.

"A freaking prince," she said to the fake flower arrangement on the dresser. It was dust-free, and she wondered if she'd be the maid this summer or if Petra had someone coming in. Because if she did...Zara wanted to be around when Noah met the maid.

She actually smiled thinking about it. With her bag on the bed, she rolled her aching shoulders and stepped over to the double doors. The gauzy curtains billowed as if a bit of a breeze had come in, but Zara knew this house was locked down tight.

She flipped several switches until she found the one that controlled the ceiling fan, and then the curtains really went swish-swish-swish. She pulled them apart and unlocked the door, pushing it open in the next moment.

The warmth from the sun felt glorious on her bare arms, and she drew in another deep breath. This was definitely the best bedroom choice, as it had a small patio with a table built for two and a waist-high railing with a gate in it that led to the pool.

The aqua water undulated and sparkled in the sun, and Zara could think of nothing better than the sight before her.

Oh, yes, she could. She could imagine a situation where she lived in this beautiful mansion alone for the summer, making a battle plan for her dating game in the fall.

"Nice view, isn't it?"

Horror struck her right between the ribs at the sound of Noah's voice. She shaded her eyes as she glanced around, finally finding him on the second-floor balcony to her right.

"I'm surprised you came outside," she called back. "What if a reporter has a camera on a drone?"

His eyes flew to the skies, and she giggled as he ducked back under the eaves of the house, moving all the way out of sight a moment later. She heard him say, "You think you're so funny," before a door closed.

Zara did think she was funny. And now she knew how to get Noah out of her hair should he ever annoy her.

Ever annoy her? He'd annoyed her from the moment they'd met.

"Playboy," she said to the pool. "A playboy prince." Which was exactly the last thing Zara needed in her life —even if he did have gorgeous hair and eyes and a smile that had probably cost the king several thousand dollars.

And he wasn't going to stop her from having the summer of her life. She owned no less than ten swimming suits, and she went back into her bedroom and changed into one she didn't use for work. Pairing that with a billowy, white coverup, she padded down the hall and around the corner and down another hall into the kitchen to see what Prince Noah had to drink in the fridge.

She'd definitely be getting her steps in just by traveling from her room to the kitchen for meals. The fridge was easily ten feet wide, with huge double doors that swung all the way open. Zara felt like she was standing in front of the refrigeration units at the convenience store as she took in the bottles and cans before her.

"At least he has good taste in beverages," she said, selecting a bottle of pomegranate lemonade.

Down the halls, around the corners, and out the doors, Zara positioned herself beside the pool, her lemonade and her phone all she needed to watch the sun set into the Pacific Ocean in front of her.

And it didn't matter that she'd have to deal with a spoiled prince and his huge dog this summer. This place was big enough for the two of them, and if she couldn't have friends up to the mansion, so be it.

Zara liked being alone anyway.

———

THE FOLLOWING MORNING, SHE'D FED WHITEWATER AND shut her in the suite where they'd be living for the next few months. The rainfall shower head in the bathroom had been divine, and she wound her damp hair around and around into a bun as she entered the kitchen at the same time Noah slid three fried eggs onto a plate.

"Morning," he said like they'd be best friends forever

by the end of the day. "Breakfast?" He raised those deliciously thick eyebrows at her, his face a bit less clean shaven this morning.

"You cook?"

"A little," he said. "Coffee, toast, eggs, bacon. The usual suspects for breakfast."

"Then sure," Zara said, sliding onto a barstool. "I'll take an egg."

"Coming up." He set the pan back on the stove and cracked another egg into it. The satisfying hiss of the white and yolk meeting the hot pan sang through Zara's soul. So she liked to cook. It wasn't a crime, and she didn't want to be a chef at Indian Room just because she liked putting a meal together.

"So how'd you sleep?" he asked, turning from the stovetop.

She peered at him, trying to decide if he was really asking or if he knew she'd been awake half the night, wondering if he wore pajamas to bed or not.

"Fine," she ended up saying. "You?"

"Oh, it was a rough night." He ran one hand down his face, flashed her a smile, and plucked a fork from a drawer. He started cutting into his eggs, letting the yolk run out and touch his toast.

Zara almost gagged. "I like my eggs well-done," she said. She got up and rounded the island. "I can do it." She'd just picked up the spatula when he appeared at her side.

"I can do it. My mother called a well-done fried egg a

25

rubber sole." He took the spatula gently from her fingers and carefully broke the yolk, adding a bit of salt and pepper before flipping the egg with the ease of someone who'd done it a great many times before.

"Well then, I need a rubber sole." She inhaled, finding it so unfair that he could smell so good and look like he'd just tumbled out of bed moments ago. She found a hint of pine, something spicy, masculine, and a hint of fabric softener under that. Maybe the fresh breeze scent.

"Are you going down to town today?" he asked.

"Yes," she said. "It's my day off, but I'm going to give notice at my apartment and pack a few more things."

"I was thinking you could drop me off at Your Tidal Forever before you did all that."

Zara backed up a few steps, finally realizing how close they stood together. In the next moment, he turned from the stove too, the pan in his hand. He pulled down a plate with his free hand and slid the rubber sole out of the pan.

"There you go."

"Thanks." She opened the same drawer he had, grabbed a fork, then a couple slices of bacon, and retreated back to the barstool she'd been sitting on earlier.

"So today?" he asked. "I've already spoken to Shannon, and she said I can come in anytime."

"Great," Zara said, though she did not think it was

great. "We can go anytime then. Unless, of course, you were planning to shower before leaving the house."

His eyebrows puckered for a moment, and then he dropped his gaze to his food so she couldn't read it. "Maybe I should get your number," he said, ignoring her jab about showering. "Then I can let you know when I'm ready to go."

"I'm not a car service." She bit off the end of a piece of bacon, imagining it to be his head.

"Fine," he said, his dark eyes flashing dangerously. "Then when do you want to go?"

"You tell me."

"But you just said you weren't a car service."

"Because you made it sound like you'd just text me when you were ready, and I should come running out, keys ready." Zara had plenty of her own fire inside too. She tossed the half-eaten piece of bacon on her plate and stood up. "I'm going to go eat in my bedroom."

She'd taken four steps—nowhere near enough to get out of the kitchen—when he said, "Wait." He sounded a bit contrite, so Zara paused and turned back to him. "I'd still like your number, and yes, I need to shower. Maybe we could go in about an hour?"

Ah, so the prince *could* be nice. Zara smiled, hoping it came off as sweet. "Sure. I'll meet you in the car in an hour." She turned and started walking away again. She'd never be able to storm out to make a point the next time they argued. This house was too freaking big.

"What about your number?" he called after her.

"Yeah, I'm still deciding on if you need that or not." She finally reached the hallway and turned left as he started to chuckle, a sound that wormed its way under Zara's skin and into her bloodstream, no matter how much she wished it wouldn't.

An hour later on the dot, she opened the door from the kitchen to the garage to find Noah already there, the huge double-doors already open and letting in tons of sunlight.

"So how are we going to do this?" he asked, peering down through her back door windows.

"Do what?"

He straightened and faced her, and Zara's heart did a little jig in her chest. So he was extremely good-looking. Handsome. Some might even say gorgeous. *Drop-dead gorgeous*, Zara thought, her own mind betraying her.

No wonder he needed to do some volunteer work to repair his image. He probably had women throwing undergarments at him, and he probably hadn't resisted all that much.

She shook her head, trying to clear the thoughts. She didn't know him, and it wasn't right of her to make such assumptions about him just because she'd read a paragraph off the Internet about him and his royal status.

"I can't be seen coming and going from here," he said. "People have to think you're house-sitting."

"Oh, right." Zara glanced around the garage, but it was like the prince and his family didn't really live here.

"Do you have any blankets or anything? We could pile those on top of you."

Inside the house, his dog barked, and Noah looked over her shoulder. "He has to be quiet too. If someone gets too close to the house and hears him, they'll know I'm here too."

"Are you guys like a package deal?" she asked. "Wherever you go, Lassie does too?"

Annoyance flashed across his face, but Zara didn't mind all that much. "His name's Boomer," he said icily. "And yes, he goes everywhere I do—and the paparazzi know it."

"Maybe you should've named him something like Whisper," Zara said.

Noah rolled his eyes and said, "I'll go get some blankets."

She stepped out of his way, enjoying herself a little too much. As soon as he'd gone, a knot of guilt struck her in the gut. She should be nice to him. He was obviously concerned about the media finding him, and something he'd said last night flowed through her mind.

The anonymity I've never had.

Zara's guilt doubled and then tripled, and she sighed under the weight of it. When Noah returned, she said, "Sorry for how I've been acting. I just...I was expecting to be here alone this summer."

Noah blinked at her over the pile of blankets in his arms. "You've been acting badly?"

The urge to roll her eyes was so strong, she almost

couldn't stop herself. Luckily, she did, and she stepped forward to take some of the blankets. "I have been. I'm sorry. I'm sure we'll get used to our living arrangements."

Noah put that charming smile on his face, and Zara could definitely see how he'd gotten himself into some trouble with that. "All right. Well, thank you for apologizing. Now let's see how this works."

Chapter Four

Noah was much too tall and much too broad for the backseat of a sedan. Especially the floor of a sedan. Zara had moved the passenger seat up as far as it would go, and if he put most of his weight on one arm, he could almost fit.

To cover him, though, the blankets would need to go almost all the way to the windows, and he thought that was way too obvious. And how would he get out? Spill out the door and shake off a dozen blankets like he was Boomer?

Foolishness raced through him. Maybe he should abandon this insane plan to be seen volunteering in Getaway Bay. It wouldn't create that much sympathy for him, because everyone would just leave comments like, "Oh, he has to spend his summer in Hawaii. Too bad for him."

Noah had read hundreds of sarcastic comments in his lifetime, and he didn't need any more.

"Okay," Zara said, starting to cover him with the blankets. "Are you ready?"

"Maybe this is stupid," he said. Their eyes met, and in that moment where she wasn't saying something about how he stunk because he hadn't showered or telling him he'd named his dog wrong, there was a tenderness in her gaze.

"You want to volunteer at the wedding, right?" she asked.

"Yes," he said.

"Then this is what we have to do." She started unfolding another blanket to cover his legs. "And you better text me a grocery list so we don't have to do this more than we have to."

"I'll need your number for that," he said, his heartbeat rioting the slightest bit. He wanted her number, and not just to send grocery lists. He'd lain awake in bed last night, thinking about her downstairs and wishing he could talk to her. Tell her some private, personal things about himself that he'd never told anyone before.

Because despite being wealthy and having nearly everything he wanted, Noah was desperately lonely. And sometimes, he made bad decisions just to have someone to talk to. That was all that had happened in Venice, though it certainly looked like something else entirely had gone down.

She laughed, which made Noah smile, and she said, "Oh, you're good, Mister Wales. Very slick."

"Hey, you're the one who suggested it."

She lifted a pile of folded blankets and dropped them on his head and shoulders. He grunted, but when she said, "Give me your number, and I'll text you," he decided he could handle having the blankets unceremoniously tossed on him.

He recited his number, and a few seconds later, his phone chimed and vibrated.

"That's me," she said. "Now, let's get going. This day is almost halfway over already."

The ride down the twisty, winding road from the bluff to the city seemed to take forever. Every turn put more pressure on his arm, and by the time she parked, his entire left side was numb—and he was sweating.

They hadn't spoken, so when she said, "All right. The coast looks pretty clear," her voice was muted and muffled by all the blankets. "Am I coming to let you out?"

"Yes, please," he said, his royal training kicking in. His tutors would be so proud.

"Oh, there's a couple with a dog."

Noah wanted to scream, but he held still and waited.

"Bicyclists," Zara said next, and Noah started to squirm, trying to find a position that didn't cause agony from his hip to his spine. But her floor in the back wasn't flat, and he felt like a rainbow over the hump that ran down the middle.

Finally, *finally*, the door opened, and she lifted the

blankets off his face. It was like breathing for the first time. The sun was too bright, and he squinted as he looked up at Zara. She was haloed in sunshine, and the most beautiful creature he'd ever laid eyes on. His pulse thrummed through his body, and he wondered what it was trying to tell him.

"Come on," she hissed, breaking the vision. "You can't just lie there and stare."

He wiggled his way out of the car and onto the hot pavement, jumping up a moment later and dusting off his hands. She dumped the blankets on the backseat and closed the door behind him. "Very graceful, Your Highness."

Noah froze, his heart racing around his chest for a completely different reason now. "So you know."

"I have a Smartphone," she said. "I looked you up when I was parking yesterday."

Noah clenched his teeth and pressed his lips into a tight line. "Did you recognize me?"

She scoffed like this wasn't the most important conversation on the planet. "Don't flatter yourself."

A measure of relief moved through him, especially when she said, "You gave me your name. I Googled it." She clicked her tongue as she started walking around the car to the driver's side. "You brought up *a lot* of articles, buddy."

Embarrassment heated his blood now. "Which ones did you read? Because you know, not everything on the Internet is true."

Zara laughed, the sound magical as it lifted into the sky. "I read enough to know you're a...." She glanced around and closed her mouth, thankfully. "I'll be back in a bit. You better text me what you want for lunch, and at the grocery store, okay?"

He nodded and looked out at the ocean. It had been so long since he'd actually touched an ocean despite living beside one. "Okay," he said.

She gave one curt nod like she was his nanny and slid behind the wheel. So Noah watched as her shorts hitched up a little higher on her leg. It wasn't a crime.

Zara was beautiful, with long limbs and miles of that Indian skin. Noah looked away and walked toward the boardwalk that would lead him down the beach a bit to the offices of Your Tidal Forever, hoping that by the time he called his mother that night, he had an action plan in place. Otherwise, the Queen of Triguard would dictate one for him, and Noah was much too old for that.

———

Hope Sorensen blew around the building like a tornado, and Noah kind of just wanted to stand back and watch. But she had her assistant, a curvy brunette named Shannon Bell—who Noah had communicated with the most—hand out assignments to everyone there to volunteer. Shannon put him to work on the Invitation Committee, which turned out to be the absolute worst place for him.

He didn't care what font was used on the announcements. Then he realized they hadn't even been talking about the actual announcement, but something called the "Save the Date" card that needed to be out in the next three days. Apparently, if it wasn't, the world would end. Or something.

The four women at the table with him kept looking at him as if he had something to say. So he threw out things like, "I think the cerulean is nice there," and "Honestly, I don't think the seal matters."

They took his advice on the blue, though he had no idea why, but one woman actually gasped when he said the bit about the seal. It was a sticker, for crying out loud.

But Noah had never been married, so clearly he didn't understand the importance of pictures, and colors, and stickers. Oops, seals.

His mother would be all over this, and Noah found himself thinking of her a lot during the two-hour meeting.

Then he got put on something he could actually get behind. Addressing envelopes. It was boring, tedious work. Every time he messed up and had to reposition a sticker, he felt a bit bad at wasting the paper. But at least he could see something getting done.

In Noah's opinion, there was absolutely nothing worse than a meeting. He was convinced the good Lord had invented them just to torture men like him.

Now, his father adored a good meeting, which summed up exactly how different Noah was from his father, the King of Triguard. About the only thing they had in common was the fact that they both wanted the Queen to be happy.

And there was that thought of his mother again. Noah would call her as soon as he got back to the privacy of the house.

With the thought of the mansion, his thoughts turned to Zara. An exasperated sigh slipped from his lips, and he hadn't even seen her for hours. He just wanted some time to himself. Time to figure out why he still didn't know what to do with his life after thirty-one years.

But her being the house sitter would testify that the house was indeed empty. And the mansion was *huge*. Noah could probably go days without having to see her, and he just might.

"Those look great," Hope said when she buzzed into the room. Four long tables had been set up and no less than ten people worked to type in addresses, print them on labels in a font that had taken fifteen minutes to choose.

"You went with Desire?" Hope asked, picking up one of the ivory envelopes. "And are these from our scented line?" She brought the paper to her nose. "Ah, yes. Vanilla crème."

Noah stared at her, sure she was joking. But the small smile on her face wasn't of the kidding kind.

He tuned out the redhead who explained how the decision to use the font had transpired, and instead focused on getting that return address label exactly squared away in the corner of the vanilla crème envelopes.

This wedding was actually the union of two celebrities, one of whom lived right here on the island. Apparently Collin Marsh was a huge action star, and he was marrying a woman from one of those reality TV shows.

So the island would be crawling with reporters. Thankfully, those who wanted pictures of a prince from a tiny island in the Greek Isles didn't usually run in the same circles as those capturing Hollywood stars.

He thought he'd be okay. He hoped. He'd actually prayed for it while he was underneath those blankets, coming down off the bluffs in the back of Zara's sedan.

With only two hundred envelopes left to stuff and label, his phone buzzed against his hip. He pulled it out and checked around the room like he was doing something wrong. But he was a volunteer; Hope couldn't fire him.

Still, all he'd ever done in his life was volunteer. Serve. He'd never had a real job to speak of, and his mother had always taught him to live in the moment. Be present. Put your phone away.

But it was Zara, and she was asking him how much longer he thought he'd be. He glanced around at this pop-up post office, and texted back, *Thirty minutes.*

I'll be straight out from the front doors, on the beach.

Noah acknowledged that he'd come find her when he got done, and promptly slid his phone back in his pocket, glad he'd made it through a four-line conversation without wanting to say something sarcastic to Zara.

Baby steps, then.

Forty-five minutes later, he'd agreed to come back on Thursday to help with the construction of...something. All he knew was that Hope had asked him to be there for something requiring hammers, saws, and a nail gun.

He was all over that, as the castle at Triguard had a crew of six gardeners and four maintenance men, and the closest he ever got to building something was when he tried to fix some stupid misunderstanding between him and the rest of the world.

He left Your Tidal Forever in favor of the hot afternoon sun. It actually soothed him as his dark skin drank it up, and he sighed. He found Zara on the beach all right, wearing a black swimming suit that showed the entire length of her toned, tanned legs.

She carried a beat-up surfboard under one arm as she laughed with another man.

Something hot and spiked roared through Noah, and he paused, still back on the loose sand. Who was that guy? Did Zara have a boyfriend?

Why Noah hadn't thought a woman as beautiful as Zara wouldn't, he wasn't sure. But the thought had never crossed his mind.

It was crossing it now, and Noah didn't like it. Not one little bit.

So he was jealous. Didn't mean he wanted a new relationship with the gorgeous Zara Reddy. It just meant he was a male and had happened to notice that Zara was an attractive female.

After all, they didn't get along, and her having a boyfriend would actually be a good thing. Maybe then, she'd leave him alone in the mansion.

Maybe then, he could stop thinking about her.

Chapter Five

"Hey, do you give lessons?"

Zara turned toward the man asking the question, saying, "Yeah, sure, all the—" She cut off when she saw it was Noah. She cursed herself for speaking so quickly. Her exuberance to book another job—anything that made money and kept her out of the restaurant— had cost her this time.

"I mean, not anymore." She gave him a tight, closed-mouth smile as he approached. It was wholly criminal how good he looked wearing a pair of sunglasses, his hands all tucked in his pockets like they were.

"Too bad," he said, staring out over the beautiful, teal water of the East Bay. "I've always wanted to learn how to surf."

"You grew up on an island and don't know how to surf?" Zara stared at him, disbelief racing through her. "That's just wrong."

"The water's not exactly the same," he said, glancing in her direction. She couldn't see his eyes, but she was sure he was glaring. The heat of his look seared her, so her assumption had to be right.

He seemed to be focused on Burke, and Zara startled before stepping between him and Ash's new husband. "Should we go?"

Burke edged closer though, his smile wide as he said, "Hey, I'm Burke Lawson."

"Holden Montego," Noah said, shaking Burke's hand. And the name sounded so...true. It had flawlessly slipped out of his mouth as if he'd said it thousands of times before. And Zara wondered if Noah Wales was even his real name.

Probably not, she told herself.

"Are you two together?" Noah asked, and Zara almost choked.

"No." Burke laughed and pointed down the beach a bit. "My wife is down there. She and Zara are best friends." He turned back to Noah. "But she doesn't like to surf, and Zara does, and she's nice enough to let me tag along sometimes."

"So nice," Noah said with a hugely false smile in place.

"Okay," Zara said. "Time to go."

"If he wants to surf, we could rent a board," Burke said, making things infinitely worse.

"Oh, no," Zara said, shaking her head. "No, he's not even wearing swimming trunks, and we need to get...."

She didn't know how to finish the sentence. She couldn't say "home," because then Burke would be suspicious about their living situation.

Heat flared in Zara's body, especially when Noah just stood there, mute. If he could make up pseudonyms on the spot, couldn't he come up with a reason they needed to leave the beach? Of course he could.

"Get where?" Burke asked, glancing between the two of them. He took a couple of steps closer to Zara and asked in a near-whisper, "Are you two dating?"

"What?" Zara's laughter was probably too loud. She didn't care. "No." She scoffed and shook her head, looking at Noah just standing there. "No, we are not dating. I'm just giving him a ride somewhere," she said, seizing onto the perfect excuse. "You know how I do that My Car, Your Destination thing sometimes."

A sour look crossed Burke's face. "I thought you gave that up after that guy—"

"Well, I didn't," Zara practically yelled at him, hoping he'd shut up already. The last thing she needed was Noah finding out about the incident that had ended with Zara sitting in the police station, giving statements, until three o'clock in the morning.

She met Noah's gaze, and even through those blasted mirrored shades, and she could feel his curiosity practically sizzling in the air between them.

"And we need to go." She started toward Ash, who lay on her back, a book held up in the sky over her face.

She reached her friend and said, "I'll call you later, okay?"

"Okay," Ash said, totally unconcerned.

Zara shoved her clothes in her bag and wadded up her towel under her other arm. She marched up the beach, away from her friends, without checking to see if Noah was behind her. He was. He had no other way back to the house, and he couldn't stay down in town, out in the open.

Sure enough, she'd pulled on a T-shirt and tossed her beach stuff in the backseat when he joined her. "They seem nice," he said.

"So nice," she echoed back to him in a sarcastic voice, the way he had to Burke down on the beach. She set to work tying her board to the top of the sedan, surprised when Noah helped by securing the lines on his side.

Zara snuck glances at him across the top of the car, finally finishing and saying, "Thank you." She didn't mean to sound so begrudging about it, but she couldn't suck the words back in and try again.

So she got behind the wheel of the car, and then jumped back out. "Oh. The blankets."

Noah groaned as he opened the back door, and by the time she made it around to the passenger side in the back, he was in position.

"I'm sorry," she said. "Maybe you could sit in the front and just lay your seat down."

"No, just put the blankets on, and let's go."

She worked not to throw them with all the force she had in her as she told herself that he probably didn't mean to sound so demanding. So barky, like she better jump to it with a smile on her face.

Probably, probably, probably, she told herself all the way up to the bluffs and into the garage. Then she got out and left Noah in the backseat to get himself out.

———

THE SCENT OF FRESHLY BAKED BREAD AND CINNAMON urged her awake the following morning. Zara rolled over and breathed in deep, comfortable and warm and still woozy. She'd been having the best dream about lying by the swimming pool at the mansion, a smoothie from The Straw on the ground beside her chaise.

The sun was glorious. The view even better. And then Noah had come out, bringing pizza and chocolate chip cookies for her. He'd put them on the table nearby and taken off his shirt—

Zara's eyes snapped open.

No…she had not just had a summer fantasy about Noah. The man was absolutely maddening, even if he knew his way around a kitchen.

She sat up and pushed the comforter off her legs. She wasn't even that hungry. Her stomach chose that moment to protest loudly about how long ago her last meal had been, and she reached for her phone to see how late she was.

"Only seven-thirty?" she asked as if she couldn't believe the numbers on the home screen of her phone. She had swimming practice that morning at nine, so she'd shower after work. So maybe she had time for a quick bite to eat before heading out.

The fact that she never ate breakfast...well, no one needed to know that. Especially not the handsome man standing in the kitchen, twirling a pair of tongs like they were drumsticks as he sang along with the music blasting through the house.

She leaned against the wall and watched him, a smile tugging at the corners of his mouth. So maybe he was adorable when he let go of his stuffy Prince persona. Maybe he was capable of having a conversation that didn't include sarcastic remarks and barking commands.

He flipped a few pieces of bacon and lifted the tongs to his mouth like they were a microphone.

Zara couldn't help the laugh that bubbled out of her mouth.

Noah stiffened and turned toward her, a perfectly pleasing blush entering his cheeks.

"Oh, go on," she said with a sweeping motion of her arm. "I have a feeling we were just getting to the good part."

He reached up to a speaker on top of the fridge and turned down the music. "What?"

She shook her head and kept grinning. "Nothing. Are you sure you're a prince?" She gasped, but it was obviously fake and over-the-top. "Maybe you're Prince. You know, *the* Prince. They reported that he'd passed away, but I don't know...." She cocked her head. "I think you kind of look like him."

Noah frowned, reached to turn off the burner under the bacon, and twisted away from her as he lined a plate with paper towels. "Who's Prince?"

"Oh, now that's just sad," Zara said as she moved into the kitchen and took her spot at the bar. "You don't know who Prince is?"

"No, I don't." And the barking was back.

"He's a pop star," Zara said, eyeing the cinnamon rolls and enjoying herself entirely too much. "I don't think he used tongs for a mic, though." She giggled, and Noah turned around, half a smile on his face too.

"I'm definitely not a pop star."

"What I heard goes to the contrary." This banter —*flirtatious banter?*—was better than the sarcastic jabs. At least Zara liked it better.

He set the plate of bacon on the counter and asked, "Are you eating or going?"

"Eating first," she said. "Then going. I have practice today." Then she'd bring in all the stuff she'd packed at her apartment. She had another week to get everything out, and she was planning to make several trips.

"What time are you going down on Thursday?" he asked, using a rubber spatula to retrieve a cinnamon roll from the pan.

"I have practice at nine," she said.

"Can I get a ride to Your Tidal Forever?" He looked at her, and for a moment, Zara felt like she was falling.

A breath in, then out, and everything righted itself. She looked away, suddenly self-conscious with him. With her heart beating at the speed of hummingbird wings, she reached for a piece of bacon.

"Sure, yeah," she said, a nervous undertone to the words. "We'll just have to leave a little earlier. My practice facility is in the other bay."

"Tell me what time," he said, the words gentle. "And I'll be ready."

Zara nodded and busied herself with bacon and frosted buns, this new energy between them completely different than before. Had he felt it too? Had she just never looked him fully in the eyes before?

She wasn't sure how she even felt, and her stomach turned over and over as she cleaned up her dishes, gathered her swim gear, and drove down to town. As she pulled into the parking lot at the amphitheater, where they'd be practicing that morning, Zara realized she'd been *attracted* to Noah.

Physically and emotionally *attracted* to him.

"Not happening," she muttered to herself as she heaved her heavy bag onto her shoulder and joined a couple of other women heading into the locker room.

So not happening.

After all, he was a prince in a country several oceans over, and she was a synchronized swimmer with a very traditional Indian family. The very idea of bringing

Noah home to meet her parents was laughable—and caused a healthy dose of fear to tumble through her. Her mother would eat Noah for breakfast.

No, she'd house sit for the summer. Keep the paparazzi away from Noah. She'd get to lie by the pool and drink her fruity smoothies and perform in her shows at night.

Noah would do…whatever Noah was doing in Getaway Bay, and then Zara's life would go back to normal.

She took a deep breath, getting quite the lungful of chlorine, satisfied with this new plan no matter how much her heart wailed at her to *please give Noah a chance.*

Do you want to get broken? she asked it as she changed into her dark blue practice suit and made sure she had her goggles and nose clips. *Because that's what'll happen. Men like Noah…they break hearts.*

Her pulse finally settled after that, and she could focus on what she needed to do that day—master the three-sixty leg kick while wearing heels in the swimming pool. She definitely didn't have room for Noah Wales in her brain too.

Chapter Six

Noah checked all the Internet gossip headlines, and he only found one talking about him and Katya. Nothing he hadn't seen or read before, even if none of it was true. Truth didn't matter on the Internet, nor to the "journalists" that reported on celebrity news.

This particular one had been on his tail for a decade, and Noah was honestly surprised he'd been able to sneak out of Venice without the guy knowing or following him. Tomas seemed to know where Noah was before Noah himself had a plan.

He stood at the sliding glass doors in his suite, looking out at the ocean. He had always wanted to learn to surf, and he'd been doubly excited to learn if Zara would be the teacher.

"And that makes no sense," he murmured to his faint reflection in the window. He couldn't even step out onto the balcony and breathe in the Hawaiian air. No, he hadn't seen any drones out. No one sniffing around the house. Nothing.

Of course, he hadn't left the house for more than the few hours he'd gone down to Your Tidal Forever, and then a few minutes on the beach. No one had recognized him. Of course, all the people at the wedding planning business had been so focused on the tasks they were doing for the Marsh wedding, and people at the beach didn't care who else was there.

Noah had the strangest urge to leave this house. He'd never had a problem being confined to a castle before; he'd done it many times. He'd been late to a few interviews because he was working with the Grandparents Patrol in Triguard. The reporters had been rude, and Noah may have snapped back at them.

It was something no one else in his family would've done. They would've smiled and apologized, answered all the questions, and kept the family's public image through the roof. Noah was obviously the black sheep. The bad boy.

He shook his head. After that incident and the multiple articles that had been printed about his "short fuse," he'd started to work at the library with underprivileged children in the country, as well as keep his hours with the elderly.

That had gone well, and he'd managed to build back up most of his image. He didn't mind the work, but he felt like he wasn't really doing anything with his life. Damien, his older brother, would take over the kingdom, and he was practically perfect in every way. But he didn't spend hours and hours volunteering the way Noah did.

His sister Louisa dealt with a lot of the same pressures as Noah, but she was prim and proper and actually liked it. She had a serious boyfriend she'd been dating for five years, and the wedding plans had been in the works for a solid eighteen months.

Noah hadn't received a Save the Date for his own sister's wedding, which meant it was still months away. He had no doubt Louisa would tie the knot with Eric Newman, because they were a smart match—and they loved each other.

Noah had wondered many times over the years if he'd ever find someone he could love. He'd considered leaving the island country where generations of Wales had been born and raised and going to America, finding a job, and living a more normal life. No one would recognize him, and he'd find someone to live the rest of his life with, the way they did in those romance movies his mom loved so much.

He sighed and turned away from the window. Boomer barked, and Noah rolled his eyes. "Come on, then," he said and opened the bedroom door. Boomer scampered through door, his claws clicking on the tile in the hall. He ran downstairs, and Noah supposed his bathroom needs were quite urgent.

Following, he paused just before the door and opened it a crack. Boomer nosed his way out, and Noah stayed out of sight. If there was someone around and they saw his dog, though, they might as well have seen him.

He could probably go outside just for a few minutes while his dog took care of business. He did, his bare feet touching the grass and found it hot. Of course, it would be hot. It was June in Getaway Bay, in the middle of the day, and everything was hot.

He tipped his head back and looked into the sky, taking a deep breath of the stale, heated air. It wasn't that much better out here than inside, but he somehow didn't feel as caged.

Inside, a door slammed. Boomer barked and headed back in, and Noah turned that way too. "It's just Zara," he said to the dog, but Boomer barked a couple more times and then Zara started giggling.

The sound wormed its way right under his skin, heating his blood and making his pulse accelerate. He stepped over to the door and peered in to see her kneeling down, scrubbing Boomer's back and telling him what a good boy he was.

How would she even know?

But Noah enjoyed watching her, and Boomer obviously liked the attention. He licked her face, and she laughed again.

"How was practice?" he asked as he stepped inside and brought the door closed behind him.

"Oh." Zara quieted and stood up. She picked up her bag, and it looked like it was heavy. He wondered how much swimming suits and swim caps could weigh, but he didn't say anything. What he wanted to say, he couldn't.

If I asked, would you go to dinner with me?

Number one, they couldn't leave the house to go somewhere on the island. With all the modern apps, he could get anything delivered to the house. Well, Zara could. He didn't want to call and order anything, nor answer the door. So trying to have a romantic dinner with her would be impossible.

The fact that he *wanted* to have a romantic date with her was insane. Completely insane.

"What's your show called?" he asked next, because she hadn't answered his first question and she stood there, staring at him.

"Fresh Start," she said.

"Anyone can get tickets?" He took another step closer, his eyes locked onto hers. Hers were dark with hints of gold, and he wanted to dive in and bask in the warmth of them.

"Well, yes," she said, backing up against the island in the kitchen. "But we've been sold out for a while."

Sold out? Noah blinked, sure he could find tickets somewhere. "Do you get any tickets?"

"Yes," she said slowly, still looking at him. "But my family is using them."

"Of course," he said, backing up and giving her a little space.

"You wouldn't be able to come anyway," she said, tracking his movement as he edged away from her.

"I wouldn't?"

"Am I going to smuggle you down?" She blinked at him. "You don't leave the house."

"I'm thinking I might be okay," he said.

"It's been three days."

"I've actually been here for five days." Noah didn't know why he was arguing this point with her. "And I've worked at Your Tidal Forever. No one even looked at me." He'd been just another body, like always.

No one wanted Noah Wales front and center. He was the throw away. The leftover. The one the C-list reporters wanted interviews with, hoping to catapult themselves up to the King or Queen.

"So you think you can start socializing in town?" Zara gaped at him.

Foolishness raced through him, and he wanted to end this conversation. He'd walked away from a few conversations in his life, but he didn't think he could just turn his back on Zara. She had enough fire to come after him, shouting to be heard if she had to.

"I don't know what I think," he said. "Forget I said anything." He tossed her a look over his shoulder as he left the kitchen. "Come on, Boomer." At least the dog came with him, still knowing where his loyalty should be.

Noah went back upstairs, but there was absolutely nothing for him there. Problem was, Zara was downstairs, and that meant there was definitely nothing for him down there either.

Except a ride back down to Your Tidal Forever in the morning. He could survive until morning. He could.

Couldn't he?

————

WHEN HE WALKED INTO YOUR TIDAL FOREVER, HE nearly got knocked back out of the door by the sheer amount of estrogen hanging in the air. He paused, wondering why he'd come here today.

Riley, a cute redheaded woman, stood from her desk in the lobby. "Hello, Holden. We've got the construction crew meeting across the boardwalk at the rehearsal hall." She flashed him a professional smile, her heels clicking as she moved toward him. She stepped past him and pushed open the door. "See? Right there."

Noah could see it. "Great, thanks." He flashed her a smile, and she cocked her head.

"Do I know you?"

Noah kept his royal smile in place. "I don't think so. I'm new in town."

"And you're volunteering here?"

"Yes." He looked over her shoulder. "I'll head over there now. Thanks." He worked hard not to punch his way through the glass door in his haste to get away from Riley. Thankfully, she let him go, and Noah kept his back straight and his strides even as he walked down the sidewalk.

He wanted to bolt as fast as his feet would go. But he

also wanted to see what it took to build an altar and a trellis and a custom buffet.

Thankfully, the first thing someone did when he entered the event hall was hand him a pair of goggles. He slipped them on, glad for the extra layer of anonymity.

A man who was clearly in charge came over. He glanced at his clipboard. "Holden?"

"That's right," Noah said.

"I'm Cal." He glanced over his shoulder. "This says you don't have experience with power tools."

"Nope," Noah confirmed.

"Then I'll have you on supplies. This way." Cal wove through the other men working with saws and nail guns, and Noah wished he'd told a little fib. It didn't look that hard to hold a nail gun in place and push a button.

Pop, pop, pop! went the nail gun, and the man turned the two pieces of wood he was holding.

"I'm going to pair you with Ed. He's building the lattices, and he'll need a runner." He pointed to a huge pile of thin strips of wood. "Ed's the big guy with the yellow shirt on. His last name's Lemon, and I've never seen him without the color yellow somewhere." With that, Cal left Noah to find Ed and figure out how often he'd be running back and forth between this pile and the man in the yellow shirt.

Ed was just inside the door, and Noah stepped over to him and introduced himself with his false name. "Ed Lemon." He held a staple gun that looked like a toy in his huge hands. "We're making sixteen trellises." He gestured behind him to where something leaned against the wall.

The thin pieces .of wood had been stapled to the frame in a lattice pattern, and Noah was actually surprised he knew such a thing. "Sixteen of these?"

"And then we'll be painting them."

Noah stepped over to the completed trellis and saw all the ninety-degree angles. "Might it be easier to paint them before stapling them together?" He could only imagine how the paint would pool in the creases, and it would definitely be easier to swish color on up and down, up and down, before nailing them all together.

"I suggested that too," Ed said. "But apparently, the bride doesn't want the staples to show." He stapled another thin strip to the one underneath it. "I showed Hope that these staples disappear, but I was vetoed." He nodded to the corner. "We've got spray paint, so it shouldn't be terribly hard."

He stapled again and then again. "So you'll bring me the wood pieces, move the trellises, and once we've got a good system going, you can paint too."

Noah wasn't sure about the painting, but he nodded as if he'd been a construction manager his whole life. "Great. Looks like what? Fifteen across? Twenty down?"

"Twenty-five down," he said, stapling.

"The frame is thicker." Noah hadn't seen any thicker wood.

Ed nodded his chin toward a stack of wood Noah hadn't seen. "That's there."

Noah felt like he knew what he needed to do, and now he just had to hop to it. It looked like Ed had all the wood he needed to finish the trellis on the table, and Noah headed outside to start bringing in the forty lengths of wood Ed would need for trellis number three.

Noah worked up a sweat walking back and forth, and Ed had the trellis built before Noah had all the wood in. He took the trellis and leaned it against the first one. Ed moved with the speed of a Tasmanian devil, and he had the thicker frame put together while Noah had only one more load of wood to bring in.

"What do you do for a living?" he asked Ed.

"Oh, I'm a surgeon," he said, glancing away from his work for a moment. "You?"

"Uh…." Noah had no idea what to say. He had a fake name, but he hadn't thought much farther ahead than that.

Ed stapled and picked up another board, positioning it right along the marks he'd made with a pencil.

"I'm a director," Noah said.

"Sounds made up." Ed gave him a smile that said he knew Noah had just lied to him.

"Why are you here stapling a trellis together if you're a surgeon?" Noah asked.

"The hospital here requires us to donate a certain number of hours to the community," Ed said. "Most doctors do pro bono care, but I do reconstructive surgery.

So." He shrugged. "Plus, this gets me out doing something I don't normally do."

Noah left and brought in another load of wood. "You seem pretty handy."

"I've built a few things," Ed said. "A gazebo in my backyard. A tree house for my nephew. That kind of stuff."

Noah could spend time with people, reading with kids or playing chess with someone's grandfather. But he didn't really have any employable skills. Maybe he should spend his time learning how to build things instead of something like surfing.

But then you can't get Zara to help you.

He shook the thought away, but it didn't go far, and by the time all sixteen trellises were finished, he'd decided to see if she'd at least be willing to drive him down to town for a lesson with someone else.

Chapter Seven

Zara squared her shoulders as she pulled into the parking lot at Indian House. She'd had a long day of practice, and Noah had filled her whole car with the scent of sweat and sawdust, and she was having a very hard time keeping him out of her mind.

He'd asked her to teach him to surf again, and Zara had said she had to get down to talk to her father at the restaurant, and she'd bolted back to the garage.

So now, here she sat, outside the restaurant her parents owned, wondering if she could handle going inside. She hadn't seen her mother in about a week, which meant Zara would need to be ready to defend her single status.

Her stomach grumbled, because Ian had made them work through half of their lunch, dissatisfied with the way the formations on the island that came up out of the water looked. So she killed the engine and headed for the entrance.

It was almost the weekend and right during the dinner rush, which was actually perfect. Then her siblings would be busy, and she wouldn't have to be crammed into a booth for four with all five of her sisters.

The bell rang as she opened the door, and Abi, the hostess looked up. Her whole face brightened, and she said, "Zara." She put the menu back in the holder on the front of the podium, and said, "Mom and Dad just sat down for dinner. You want to join them?"

Zara's heart sank, but she painted a plastic smile on her face and said, "Sure." She gave Abi a big hug, as her older sister was actually one of the more sane members of her family. As Abi led her through the dining room, she caught sight of her youngest sister, Myra, standing at a table, her left hand out for the patrons to admire her new engagement ring.

Zara turned away, her throat dry and her heart suddenly beating at triple-time. Coming here was definitely a mistake.

But her mother had caught sight of her, and she exploded out of the booth, her sari catching as she stood. "Zara." She wrapped Zara in her arms, the smell of fresh cotton and Indian spices meeting Zara's nose. "What are you doing here? You look so good."

"Hey, Mom." She slid into the booth first and another of her sisters asked her what she wanted to drink.

"Just water," Zara said. Swimming in water all day really dehydrated her, and she tried to stick to water during the day and coffee in the morning. While Krisha went to get the drinks, her mom scooted into the booth.

"Still swimming?"

"Every day, Mom."

"We're coming to the show on opening night." She gave her father a look. "Right, Samir. Aren't we so excited to see Zara's show?"

"Of course," her dad said. "Only one month to go." He beamed at her. He'd had a difficult time when Zara had told him she would not be working in the restaurant, though Zara wasn't sure why. All five of her sisters worked here, as well as two brothers-in-law. They didn't need her.

"One month," Zara said as Krisha put her water on the table. "I want the butter chicken, Kris. With extra naan."

Krisha smiled at her and said, "Coming right up."

"So," her mother said. "Are you seeing anyone?"

Zara rolled her eyes and swung her head toward her mother. "No, Mom."

"No one?" Her mom had the best puppy dog eyes on the planet, and they could morph into a pool of disappointment in mere moments.

"Well, I met someone," Zara said, the image of Noah entering her mind. She couldn't believe she was still talking. "But I'm not sure about him."

"Not sure?" her mother practically shrieked. "What are you not sure about?"

So many things. "Well, Mother, for one, he's not Indian."

Her mom looked like Zara had punched her. But what Zara was not expecting was the scoff that followed. "Oh, Zara. I gave up on you finding a nice Indian man about five years ago."

"Really?"

"Really. You just need *some*one."

It was Zara's turn to scoff, and she had never been happier to see Krisha approaching with her parents' food. Because now she knew her mom would probably marry her to anyone. After all, it didn't matter if he was a nice man, or employed, or anything.

She just needed *someone*.

Disgust filled her, but thankfully, the butter chicken came next, and Zara decided she could deal with Noah and if he even qualified as *someone* after she ate.

———

When she entered the mansion, the scent of butter chicken came with her. She put the to-go container on the counter, noting that there was no dog running to see her and barely any lights on. Had Noah gone to bed already? It was barely eight o'clock. Perhaps he'd worked hard at Your Tidal Forever today.

Zara moved down the hall and into her suite to feed Whitewater. The cat wouldn't even come out from her hiding place, but somehow the food disappeared every day.

Back in the kitchen, indecision raging through her. She wanted to see Noah, because he was handsome and someone to talk to. Then she wouldn't have to be alone. She didn't want to see Noah, because they'd probably end up arguing anyway.

In the end, she ended up sending him a simple text. *Brought you some butter chicken from Indian House. If you want it.*

She'd barely taken a breath when he responded with *Be right down.* In the next moment, she heard Boomer bark, and the dog made it down to the kitchen a full minute before his owner. And when Noah walked in, his hair was damp and he wore a pair of gym shorts and a T-shirt that was obviously two sizes too small.

He grinned at her and smoothed his hair back while Zara stared at him. "Is this it?" He indicated the container on the counter, picking it up before she could answer. "Mm, smells heavenly."

"Well, Bill is the best Indian chef on the island." Zara took the end barstool where she'd been sitting whenever she ate in the kitchen.

Noah pulled open a drawer and selected a fork before coming around and joining her. He left one stool in between them, but they still sat plenty close together. "Is Bill a brother?" he asked, opening the container.

"Brother-in-law," she said. "A very nice Indian man." She wasn't sure if she succeeded in saying it normally or not. She'd been making sarcastic remarks about how her mother wanted her to find *a nice Indian man* for years now.

She turned when she felt Noah's stare on the side of her face. "We don't like Bill?" He popped a bite of chicken and rice into his mouth.

Zara looked away. "I like Bill fine."

"I detected some sarcasm there."

"My mother's been badgering me to find *a nice Indian man* for a while now," she admitted.

Noah started nodding while he finished chewing. "Oh, I get that."

"Do you?"

"Are you kidding? I'm the bad boy prince. My mother's been after me to find someone 'normal' and 'nice' for years." He chuckled, though it sounded strained around the edges. "No one I date will be good enough for her."

"Do you date a lot?" Zara asked, wondering where the question had come from.

"A little," he said, his voice full of hedging.

"Oh, come on," she teased. "A tall, strapping prince like you? Surely more than a little."

He choked on his food and reached for a napkin. "Strapping?" he pushed out of his mouth.

"How many hours a day do you work out?" she challenged.

"I work out enough," he said, dodging the question.

She laughed, glad they weren't arguing. "I'm sure you

do." She stood up, hoping to leave while they were still on good speaking terms. "Well, I'm tired."

"Hey," he said before she'd taken one step. "I signed up for some surfing lessons at the yacht club. Could you drop me off in the morning before your practice?"

Zara's veins filled with ice, and she turned back to Noah. "Surfing lessons at the yacht club?" Oh, no, that would not do. She knew who did those lessons, and Mike Wadsworth wouldn't be able to get someone like Noah to stand up on a board. Ever.

Someone with his height needed a custom board and individualized lessons.

"Yeah," he said easily, forking up more food. "I can hang around until you're done with your work."

"Hang around where?"

"Wherever." He waved his utensil like there were dozens of people he could go visit.

"You're not worried about being seen?"

A flash of worry crossed his face, but he shrugged. "A little bit," he admitted.

Zara retraced her steps and leaned against the counter. "I can teach you to surf."

Noah's dark eyes glinted like stars in a midnight sky. "You can?"

"The yacht club is inferior," she said. "I don't want you to think we here in Getaway Bay don't know how to surf." The fact that she'd mentally labeled herself as part of the local crowd and him as a newcomer to the island didn't escape her.

You're being stupid, she told herself while she waited for him to say something. Even if she taught him to surf, he didn't live here. He was only on the island until whatever storm he'd created for himself blew out.

And then he'd be gone, disappearing as easily as the sun sank into the ocean each evening.

Chapter Eight

Noah couldn't stop eating the butter chicken. Problem was, Zara was standing there, all curvy and delicious and being so nice, and she was waiting for an answer.

"This is great food," he said.

She cocked her hip and folded her arms. So he would not be telling her he'd found a pair of tickets to her show on opening night. At least not tonight.

"Fine," he finally said. "I can cancel at the yacht club. But when do you think you'll have time to teach me how to surf?" He lifted his eyebrows. "You work a lot, you know."

"Some of us have bills to pay," she shot back. "And the best time to surf is as the sun comes up." She started toward the hallway again, and Noah wanted to call her back. "So be ready at five-thirty, okay?" She tossed him a grin over her shoulder as she reached the arched doorway.

"Zara?" he asked, not sure what to say to get her to stay. He only knew he didn't want to eat alone.

She twisted back to him. "Yeah?"

"Did you...?" His mind blanked, something it literally had never done before. He always knew how to get a woman to come sit by him, smile at him, spend time with him. But Zara was so different in so many ways.

Everything he wanted to suggest required that they leave the mansion. Sit by the pool. Go on a walk. Grab breakfast after the surfing lessons. He couldn't say any of those.

"Maybe we could watch a movie tonight," he suggested, stuffing the last of his butter chicken and rice into his mouth. He watched her eyes widen, her surprise palpable. Honestly, he was a bit stunned he'd said the words too.

He was even more shocked when she said, "Yeah, all right. I just need to go change." She gave him another smile and left the kitchen.

Noah's heart started partying in his chest, and he worked to keep it in check. It was a movie. In the mansion. Still, he could make popcorn, and he jumped up from the counter, tossed his empty container in the trash and his fork in the sink, and started opening cupboards.

Surely his mother kept popcorn in this place. It took

him several minutes, but he finally found some in the cupboard above the microwave. It was ninety-nine-percent fat free, but Noah had put butter on his grocery list, and he could spruce up this diet popcorn in no time.

Ten minutes later, with his sweet and salty popcorn in tow, he stepped out of the kitchen and almost ran Zara right over. "Oh, hey," he said, stepping back. "I have popcorn, and there's a mini-fridge outside the theater room. I'm sure there are drinks in there."

She looked from him to the popcorn, her hair hanging over her shoulder. It was the first time he'd seen her with her hair down, and…he looked closer at her. She'd put on a bit of makeup too, her eyes pulling at him until he realized he was leaning forward.

"What kind of movies do you like?" she asked as he got himself moving toward the steps that went down into the basement.

"I'm flexible," he said, which caused her to laugh.

"Is that so?" she asked from behind him. "Because I've seen you sandwich yourself in my backseat, and I gotta say, I don't think you are."

"Ha ha," he said, elated that this conversation was going so well. "You know what I mean."

"So if I say I don't want to watch something where everything explodes, you'd be okay with that?"

"Sure," he said, reaching the bottom of the steps and appreciating the cooler temperatures down here. He hadn't realized he was so dang hot. Had to be the popcorn, and he shifted the warm bowl from one hand to the other.

He glanced around. "Let's see. Movies over there. Fridge here." He stepped over to it, praying with everything in him that there would be something delicious to drink inside, and pulled open the door.

Jackpot. "Yep, there's flavored lemonades in here. And a couple of sodas. Bottled water."

"I'll take water," she said.

"No lemonade?" He tossed her a look out of the corner of his eye to find her examining the shelves holding the movies.

Their eyes met, and Noah felt like he'd been caught in an alien tractor beam. "There's peach and strawberry," he said, his voice almost robotic. "Raspberry. Mango."

She grinned, her white teeth distracting him. "Fine. I'll take the mango." She looked back at the movies, breaking the connection between them. Noah felt like he was on a roller coaster, and he wondered if she had any inkling of the same.

He knew he was attractive, but did *she* find him... attractive? Could she possibly like him?

He slammed the fridge closed and turned away from her, the same way he wished he could turn away from his thoughts. He wasn't a permanent resident of Getaway Bay, and he had no plans to become one. She lived here year-round.

He was a royal, albeit from a small island. Her family

had strong cultural values he had no idea about. There was no way they could be together. And yet, Noah wanted to *try*.

It was the strangest thing, because Noah didn't have to try to do a whole lot of anything, especially when it came to women.

"I can't pick," she said, sidling up beside him. He startled, getting a nose full of her unique smell. Almost like being at the swimming pool, but with a definite hint of something like a Hawaiian floral lei.

"So let's play a game," he said, turning away from her before he could do something stupid, like kiss her. "We close our eyes and pick. We each get a turn, and we have to pick one of them."

Her eyes danced, and Noah felt that sparking attraction in every cell in his body. His hand moved toward hers, and he brushed his fingers against hers. "Deal?"

She settled her weight on her back leg, effectively putting more distance between them. "Deal."

He set down the popcorn and drinks and clapped his hands together. "All right, then. Let's see what we've got here." He moved over in front of the shelves of movies. Knowing his mother, she'd probably had the maid organize them alphabetically.

"No peeking," Zara said, jumping in front of him. She was tall, but not quite to the height of Noah. She grinned up at him and shook her head, her wavy hair swinging with the movement.

"Like you didn't just stand over here and look through them all," he said.

"Close your eyes and pick," she said.

Noah snapped his eyes shut and lifted his hand, almost hoping Zara wouldn't move out of the way. But he didn't touch her, but the hard cases of the movies. He let his fingers trail along them, then moved them down, finally grabbing onto one, slim case and gripping it.

"This one."

She snatched it from him and said, "All right. My turn."

"Wait. What did I get?" He tried to see it, but she hid it behind her back. Her grin could easily be classified as flirtatious and playful, and Noah basked in the warmth of it.

"You'll see. Now step aside."

He complied, and she closed her eyes and plucked a case from the shelves too. She held both films in her hands and said, "Okay, we've got *Sixth Sense* or *Sweet Home Alabama*." She looked up at him, and Noah honestly didn't care what they watched. He didn't think he'd even be able to pay attention.

"I'm not feeling very much like scary," he said, thinking she'd like the romantic comedy better.

"*Sweet Home Alabama* it is," she said, stuffing the other one back into a spot where it didn't belong. He grinned at it, wondering if his mother would notice next time she visited this house. Probably.

Zara took the movie, grabbed her bottle of lemonade, and headed into the theater room. Noah followed, the popcorn and his drink back in his hands. He waited for her to choose one of the recliners right in the middle of the theater, and then he sat right beside her.

"This is sweet and salty popcorn," he said. "It has sugar and salt, and it's *delicious*." He offered her the bowl, and she laughed lightly as she took a few pieces and popped them into her mouth.

A flicker of surprise flashed in her eyes, and she said, "Wow, this *is* really good." She reached over and took another handful and handed him the movie. "I don't know how to put this in."

"I got it." Noah busied himself with getting the movie going, and then he took his spot next to her again. The bowl of popcorn rested on the arms between them, and Noah really wanted to reach for a snack at the same time she did, but he didn't.

Finally, he gave up, quit eating, and moved the popcorn bowl because Zara had stopped snacking too. His pulse thundered in the vein in his neck, and he reminded himself that he'd held a woman's hand before.

Not this woman, he thought, but he employed all the bravery he could and slipped his hand over the armrests and delicately took hers.

She looked at him, but he steadfastly kept his eyes on the huge screen in front of them.

"Noah," she said.

But he squeezed her fingers and said, "Sh. This is my favorite part."

She giggled, squeezed his fingers back, and adjusted herself so he didn't have to reach quite so far to hold her hand.

Noah grinned, this level of happiness something he'd never truly experienced before.

Chapter Nine

Zara woke the next morning with the ghost of Noah's fingers between hers. When he'd reached over and held her hand, Zara had no idea what to think. She'd wanted to talk about it, but he'd playfully avoided her.

And in the end, she didn't need to discuss everything to death. He obviously felt the same current between them that she did, and he'd acted on it. Did that need to be hashed out?

After that, though, Zara had barely been able to concentrate on the movie. Her nerves marched through her body like they were on a parade route, and one of her favorite movies had passed quickly.

His hands had been full as they'd gone back upstairs, and she'd lingered in the doorway of the kitchen while he threw bottles in the trash can and rinsed out the bowl.

"See you in the morning," she'd said, taking a few steps backward.

He'd grinned and said, "Night," letting her go. She'd been glad for that, as the thought of kissing him both terrified and excited her at the same time.

She finally rolled over when her alarm went off, silencing it and getting out of bed. She yawned, the dawn not that far away, and she didn't want Noah to beat her to be ready to go. When she walked into the kitchen with her swim bag and her beach bag, she found him standing in front of the refrigerator, the door open, and the light spilling onto his face.

"Oh, you're up."

He swung the fridge closed, and even in the dim light, his gaze was powerful and penetrating. "You're late. There's no way we're making it to the beach by dawn."

Zara's shoulder ached already, and her day hadn't even started yet. But she wasn't taking "you're late" from the party boy prince. "Of course we will," she said. "If you're ready to go." She walked past him and toward the garage door.

"Oh, I'm ready."

"Great. The surf shop opens in ten minutes, and if we're lucky, we'll be the first ones through the door." She walked into the garage, Noah catching the door so it wouldn't hit her and all her bags.

He sat in the passenger seat instead of cramming himself onto the floor of the car. "Riding up here?"

"I'm going to have to go into the surf shop, right?"

"Yes. They'll have to measure you."

"Then I think I can—" His voice cut off as she backed out of the garage. "Wait."

She hit the brake, her heart thumping painfully against her breastbone. "What?"

"Pull back in."

She did.

"Close the door."

She pressed the button and the garage door rumbled closed behind the car. "We're really going to be late now."

Noah didn't answer, except to open the door and get in the backseat. "Cover me up."

Zara twisted and started tossing the blankets over the top of him. For good measure, she slid one of her bags over too. He groaned, but she ignored him. "Ready?"

"Yes." His muffled reply reminded her that there was no way she could have a normal relationship with him. The hand-holding felt stupid now, and she wished she'd ripped her fingers away from his.

With the garage open, she backed out again, this time glancing around like she expected a mob of reporters to manifest on the front lawn.

There wasn't a mob, but a single car waited at the closed gate as Zara drove toward it. "Did you see this car?" she hissed out of mostly-closed lips.

"I had a feeling," he said, and Zara kept going toward the gate, even though the two vehicles couldn't pass on this private drive.

The other car backed up and pulled to the side like they'd have a friendly chat. Zara opened the gate and eased through, indeed stopping beside the other car. She pulled a little too far forward, so her window was nearly past his.

The man behind the steering wheel looked at her behind mirrored shades. He was definitely a reporter, and a tremor of unease ran through Zara. She watched the gate close behind her and then she said, "Can I help you?"

"Do you live here?"

"No," she said, wondering how much to tell him. She had the inexplicable urge to blurt out everything, but she held her tongue and watched this guy right back.

"Do you know the people who do live here?"

"No," she said. "I was hired to housesit, so that's what I'm doing."

"So the house is empty."

"Well, except for me, yes." Something bumped the back of her seat, and she didn't appreciate Noah kicking her. What didn't he like? What did he want her to say? And how was she supposed to know with just a tap?

She inched forward again. "I'm late for work. This is private property."

"Of course."

Zara pulled forward, very slowly, relieved when the reporter made a three-point turn and followed her down the tree-lined lane.

"He's following us," she said, her eyes glued to the rearview mirror and refusing to move her lips.

"Then go to work," Noah said, his voice barely audible.

"I'm about three hours early," she said. Zara wasn't even sure she'd be able to get in the pool. An idea formed in her mind, and she seized onto it. "I'll go to the community pool. Pretend like I have to do an early-morning workout before my practice today."

Her stomach buzzed with nervous energy, and she didn't like it. Noah couldn't just stay in the car. It was warm already even though the sun was barely starting to rise. No way he could lay under all those blankets for very long.

"Do you think he'll follow me around all day?" she asked.

"What did he look like?"

Zara described the dark-haired man, how combed back and slick his hair was, the neatly trimmed goatee, and the dark olive skin—like Noah's.

"That's not Tomas," he said, and Zara didn't know if that was good or bad. "What's he driving?"

"Sleek, black luxury car."

"Any flags?"

"Flags?" She checked the rearview mirror. "No." He didn't ask another question, and Zara wound down to the stop sign at the bottom of the bluff. She looked both ways and turned left, looking behind her more than in front.

"He turned the other way." She'd never felt such relief in her life, and she almost drove right off the road.

"Where can we go to talk?" Noah asked.

"I don't know."

"You've lived here your whole life, and you don't know where we can go?"

Zara wanted to pull off the road and leave him behind. Her life was so much simpler when she just had to manage her practice schedule and lay by the pool. Everything had become so complicated the moment she'd entered that mansion and heard Boomer barking at her.

Or maybe the complications had begun when she'd started thinking she and Noah could have a relationship. When had that happened, exactly?

"Zara?" he asked, and she had the distinct impression it wasn't the first time.

"Let me drive for a minute," she clipped out between her clenched teeth, her fingers clutching the steering wheel. She headed out on the highway that led to the cattle ranch, leaving behind the pool and the best surfing spot on the island. But at least that black car wasn't following her anymore.

She finally pulled off the road and into a tiny parking lot covered in sand. Her feet slipped on the loose particles as she rounded the car and opened the back door for Noah. She tossed her bag off and pushed the blankets back. He tumbled out onto the asphalt, his breath puffing out of his mouth.

He stood and brushed his palms down his chest and thighs. "I can't breathe back there." He ran his hands through his hair, exhaled again, and paced away from her.

"The beach down there is private," she said, following him. Down a set of steps, her feet met the beach, and when she glanced behind her, she couldn't see the car. So anyone driving by wouldn't be able to see her or Noah, but they would be able to see the car....

She pushed the thought out of her head. She was allowed to come to the beach, and Noah could take off running as if he were a jogger. Just to be sure, she mentioned her idea to Noah, and he nodded a couple of times.

Zara paused next to him, both of them facing the ocean as the sun rose higher into the sky. She really hadn't thought this would be their morning on the beach. In her mind, it had been much more romantic, with him shirtless, and both of them getting pushed and pulled by the warm waves. Laughter, and sunshine, and she could admit she'd thought about kissing him before driving him back up to the mansion and then heading to work.

"Do you think that was a reporter?" she asked, deciding she could be as bold and forward as he'd been. She laced her hand through his elbow and leaned her head into his bicep.

"Yes," he said.

Is a relationship between us possible? But Zara wasn't that bold and forward, and she just let the breeze whisper between them as the minutes ticked by.

———

A COUPLE OF HOURS LATER, ZARA PUSHED INTO THE locker room, her shoulders just as tired as they'd been earlier that day. She and Noah had just stood on the beach for a few minutes, and then he said he'd try to figure out who it was so she'd know what to watch out for.

She wasn't sure why they needed a private place to have that kind of talk, but Zara couldn't figure out a lot about Noah. Pushing him out of her mind, she opened her locker and started changing.

"Hey," Suzie said, spinning the dial on her own lock. "Another day in the pool." She sighed, and Zara felt like it was a heavy sigh kind of day.

"And Ian seems to be on a rampage this week."

"Right?" Suzie opened her locker and tossed her bag into it with a metallic *clunk!* "We need a fun night away from everything."

"I'd be in on that," Zara said.

"Aren't you up at that house on the bluffs?"

Before Zara could answer, Jill appeared on her other side. "I'm so late." She pulled her bleached hair up into a ponytail and whipped an elastic around it. "Has Ian said anything yet?"

"You're not late," Zara said. "We still have fifteen

minutes."

"Really?" She looked at her watch, her dark eyes searching for clarity.

"Really," Suzie said. "And we're planning a girl's night for tonight. Zee has a fancy pool up at this mansion on the bluffs."

Zara froze, her own hair still falling over her shoulders. "What?"

"I'll bring pizza," Jill said. "Can I invite my roommate? She just broke up with her boyfriend, and she needs to get out."

"Sure," Suzie said as if she owned the place.

"Guys," Zara said. "I don't know if we can go up to the house."

"Why not?" Suzie asked, already in her swimming suit, her hair ready for the cap.

Zara avoided her eye and started combing her own hair back into a ponytail. "I'm just not sure the owner would like it."

"How long are you house-sitting?" Jill asked.

"Um, until the beginning of September."

Jill paused, though she'd been sure she was running late only a minute ago. "And we can't come sit by the pool? The owner won't even know."

No, they wouldn't. And this wouldn't be the first time Zara had invited her friends to one of the fancy places she babysat while their rich owners visited their other high-end houses.

Zara had no idea what to say. Could she agree now

87

and cancel later?

"I can't tonight," she said, securing her hair. "I have something at the restaurant."

"When then?" Suzie asked, a bit of a whine in her voice.

"We could try for this weekend," Zara said. Maybe she could talk to Noah and convince him that if she had her friends up to the house, it would convince whoever was watching her that he really wasn't there.

The door to the pool opened, and Ian said, "Come on, ladies. Starting in five minutes." The heavy door swung closed with a thunk, and Zara took a deep breath.

"All right, friends." She looked at Suzie and Jill, two women she'd performed with many times. "If we make it through this, free Indian food on me."

Suzie's face split into a grin. "Deal," she said, and she practically bounced to the exit. Zara laughed and followed with much less zip in her step, though she was grateful for the friends she saw at work each day.

And tonight, perhaps they could help her figure out what to do about Noah—if she should do anything at all.

Chapter Ten

Noah felt like he'd been living underneath a storm cloud for hours. Beyond the curtains and the glass, the sky was a crystalline blue, as was the ocean on the horizon. The trees were bright green, and birds flew through the sky.

But he wasn't part of this world, but some other, alternate world where he just watched the real world pass him by.

"I can't believe this is happening," he muttered to himself. Behind him, Boomer whined, and Noah knew how he felt. At least at home, in Triguard, he could leave the castle for the grounds. Reporters didn't dare come onto the grounds, and he could wander through the trees and stay out of the public eye.

His phone buzzed, but he ignored it. Zara had said she'd check in with him later, but he honestly wasn't sure he should perpetuate anything with her. He sure did like her though, even when they argued.

But a real relationship with her would require a lot from her, and he wasn't sure she'd be willing to give it. She'd have to leave Getaway Bay. Her family. Her job.

And he didn't see that happening. Every one of those was important to her, as he'd picked up from the conversations they'd had.

Could he leave Triguard and move to Getaway Bay? He didn't hold any position in anything important in Triguard, and his mind started down paths it had never been on before.

It had been long enough that he could call his mother, and he pulled out his phone to get the unpleasant task done. He noticed that his brother had texted, which caused a heavy dose of surprise to bolt through him.

Stopped by the house today, he said. *I really thought you'd be there. Can you please check in so Mom won't call the authorities?*

He read and re-read the text, sure the words weren't right. His brother—the next King of Triguard—had flown halfway around the world to Getaway Bay to see if Noah was at the bluff house?

That couldn't be.

Why hadn't Damien pulled through the gate? He knew the code.

Noah half-shrugged. Maybe he didn't know the code. He tapped out *Calling her now,* and then dialed his mother.

She answered after only one ring with, "Noah Sven Wales." Nothing else. No demand to know where he was or when he was coming home. Of course, he hadn't expected one. Just the scathing disappointment.

"Hello, Mother," he said. "As you can see, I'm fine."

"I'm not even going to ask where you are."

"That would be great," Noah said. "And you know that nothing in the newspapers about Venice is true, right?"

"Nothing?"

"Well, I was there with a woman named Katya."

"But you didn't get married." She wasn't asking, which was comforting to Noah.

"Mom, come on. Of course not."

She sighed, and he imagined her sitting at her personal desk, her back straight, the phone held to her ear while she participated fully. She was one of the most attentive people he knew, and a twist of guilt hit him hard.

"Do I want to know what you were doing with her?" she asked.

"Nothing, Mom. She was…in trouble and needed some help. That's what I do, so I helped her."

"You helped her."

He did not appreciate the sarcasm, and honestly, he didn't expect anyone to believe him. "Yes," he said. "She had an abusive boyfriend and needed someone to keep her safe. So she stayed at my place—in her own bed—and she was supposed to leave after a couple of days."

Those days had turned into a week, and then a month, and Noah honestly didn't mind. With sudden realization, he realized he was basically doing the same thing here. Kind of.

Zara didn't need his protection or presence—if anything, that situation was reversed. But they were living in the same house, and he was thinking about kissing her....

So he'd kissed Katya. Didn't mean they'd slept together, or that he'd proposed, both things she'd either outright said or insinuated. Then the press had descended on his condo in Venice, and he'd denied everything and fled.

So the fleeing had probably canceled out the denials. Noah was used to denying things and then hiding. It was something he was actually quite good at.

"Oh, Noah," his mother said, and Noah recognized the disappointment and acceptance in the words. "So what are you doing now?"

"Just laying low," he said, turning back to the window. The glass separating him from reality seemed so thick, and he looked away again.

"Damien went to Hawaii, but he said he only found the house sitter."

Noah said nothing, not wanting to outright lie to his mother. His long hesitation obviously clued his mother into something, because she said, "Noah," with plenty of warning in her voice.

"What?" he asked.

"Where are you?"

"I'd rather not say," he said. "I'm safe, and I'm going to fix everything that happened in Venice." How, he didn't know. He couldn't retract the articles, and there was no way he could contact Katya and make her come clean.

No, Noah knew he couldn't fix anything. If he waited things out, the story would die, and no one would care what he did. He was an inconsequential prince, and he knew it.

So maybe he could make a relationship with Zara possible....

"Noah," his mother snapped, and Noah startled. He continued his conversation with his mother, but his mind never strayed far from the beautiful woman who was currently staying downstairs.

———

NOAH MET ZARA IN THE KITCHEN WHEN SHE GOT HOME from work, the sausage and green pepper pizza only minutes away from coming out of the oven. He set the salad bowl on the counter and smiled at her. "Are you hungry?"

Relief crossed her face, and a soft smile touched her mouth. "Starving." She took her place on the barstool on the end of the counter and looked at him. She'd promised her friends free food at Indian House, but Suzie had hit the water strangely during one dive and just wanted to go home.

"You've been gone for a long time today."

"Yeah." She blinked, and it took a second for her eyes to open again. They looked sleepy and Noah leaned toward her.

The timer on the oven went off, startling him back to his tasks. He got the pizza out and set the sheet pan on the stovetop. "Do you like pizza?"

"Who doesn't like pizza?"

"Well, I'm sure there are some people," he said.

Noah cut the pizza into thin rectangles and used a spatula to slide a piece onto a plate for her. He placed it in front of her and slid a fork across the counter too.

"You made this," she said, first gazing at the pizza and then him. "Like, from scratch."

"Yeah." He served himself a couple pieces of pizza and joined her at the bar, keeping that stool between them. "My nani taught me to cook, and some of my favorite times are with her in the kitchen." He flashed her a smile, comfortable with her and glad they'd figured out how to get along. "Surely you learned to cook, what with your family being in the restaurant business."

"Yes," she said. "Plenty of lessons in the kitchen."

"And you didn't like them?"

"I did, sure," she said. "I like cooking, sometimes."

"Just don't want it to be your career."

"Exactly."

Noah nodded like he understood, and on some level,

he did. After all, he had an overbearing family who expected him to play a certain role. "And how did your family take it when you became a synchronized swimmer?"

"Oh, my father was livid," she said. "My mother cried and prayed for a week straight." Zara shook her head and cut off a bite of her pizza. "Then she spent the next few years trying to match me up with nice Indian men, hoping I'd see the error of my ways." She put the pizza in her mouth and moaned. "This is *delicious*."

"Well, it's not butter chicken." Noah picked up his pizza with his hands and bit into it. But it was good. The Alfredo sauce, the sausage, the red peppers. It was like a party in his mouth, and Boomer lay on the floor, gazing up at him hopefully.

"What about you?" she asked. "Is the bad boy prince a disappointment to his parents?"

"I talked to my mother today," he said in response, as that was easier than thinking his parents were disappointed in him. "And that man who came by this morning? He was my brother."

Zara dropped her fork, the sound of metal on ceramic rattling through the whole kitchen. "He was? I talked to a man who's going to be *King*?"

Noah rolled his eyes. "He's just a guy," he said. "Like me. Except proper, and polished, and…perfect."

Zara cocked her head, the surprise gone from her face. "Perfect? Nobody's perfect, Noah." The soft, sincere way she said his name made him once again wonder if they could somehow make their two worlds into one.

"Anyway, you did a great job. He believed I wasn't here. He's on his way home."

"Are you surprised he came?" she asked.

"Actually, yes. But I haven't been in touch with my family for a couple of weeks now, and he wanted to make sure I was all right."

"That's nice of him."

"See? Perfect." Noah finished his pizza while Zara put some salad on her plate. "When we were growing up, Damien was always better at everything. Sports, school, etiquette. All of it. Except cooking. That's the one thing I was better at."

"And what about your sister?"

"Louisa is the best with the press. She works with Damien to make sure he says all the right things, and she's got her finger on the pulse of the country."

"Oh, so we like her," she said.

"I love both of my siblings," he said.

"But Louisa more than Damien."

He looked at her, wondering how she knew. "Do you have sisters you like more than others?"

"Of course," she said easily. "Krisha is my favorite. She's the oldest, and she never acts like I'm the black sheep of the family. And Abi. I like her too. She's the one who told me if I wanted to be a swimmer, I could be a swimmer."

Noah really wanted to see Zara swim, and it had

nothing to do with the swimming suit. "That's great. And you have five sisters?"

"Five sisters," she confirmed, going back to her salad. "Our house was crazy growing up. Huge family celebrations, and so much food you'd think my mom and grandmother were cooking for the whole island." She giggled and shook her head. "Our neighbors hated us, I'm pretty sure."

"Oh yeah? Loud music?"

"So loud. So much dancing."

"I'd like to see that," he said, and Zara's eyes darted to his.

"Yeah?"

"Dancing? Definitely." He toyed with the idea of telling her about the tickets he'd been able to procure. But he held onto it, his little secret for now. They were getting along so well, and he didn't want to scare her away.

"They have luau's at the cattle ranch and the pineapple plantation," she said. "We should go sometime."

"That's not Indian dancing," he said.

"No, but it's fun. Food's good too."

"I'll look into it," he said.

She finished her salad and took a deep breath. "I'm exhausted."

"So I guess no more early-morning surfing lessons." Noah watched her stand and take her dishes to the sink.

Having her on that side of the island while he sat over here was a new experience, and he liked it.

"We can go surfing," she said.

"You think so?"

"You just said that guy this morning was your brother. Not a reporter. So if you were willing to try this morning, we can go tomorrow."

"You don't mind?"

Zara regarded him, something running through her expression that he couldn't read. "I don't mind."

Noah's temperature lifted several degrees, and he grinned at her. "Five-thirty then."

She groaned, but it was playful. "Five-thirty." She turned and walked away, twisting back at the doorway, giving him a flirtatious little grin before entering the hall and leaving him sitting in the kitchen, wondering how he could make this summer fling into something more permanent.

Chapter Eleven

Z ara met Noah in the kitchen again, wondering if the man ever slept. When she asked him, he said, "Very little, actually."

"Why's that?" she asked, accepting the cup of coffee he handed her.

"My mind never shuts off," he said simply.

"There are pills for that, you know." Their eyes met, and that zing between them was almost familiar now. Hot and quick and like lightning, but familiar.

"I've heard." He nodded her toward the garage exit, and she went that way, fire erupting through her whole body when he put his hand on the small of her back and guided her through the door.

She moved on wooden legs, and he must've noticed, because he said, "Sorry," dropped his hand, and hurried around toward the passenger door.

Zara threw her bags in the backseat and got behind

the wheel. She turned on the ignition and sat there, her fingers curling around the wheel. "Noah?" she asked.

"Yeah?"

She stared through the windshield at the immaculate door leading into the house. "Are we just playing a game here?" She couldn't believe she'd asked him, but the question had been rotating through her mind for hours and hours.

He reached over and took one of her tense hands from the wheel, lacing his fingers through hers. Instant comfort spread through her, and she relaxed into the seat. "I'll be honest. I like you, and we'll probably need to take things one step at a time to make something…long-lasting work."

"How many steps do you think it'll take?"

"A lot," he said honestly.

She looked at him, and his dark eyes drank her right up. She couldn't quite get a decent breath, and she had the strangest desire to tell him things she hadn't told anyone else.

"Have you looked up anything about me?" he asked.

"Not much," she said. "Should I?"

He shook his head. "I'd rather you not." He drew in a deep breath and swallowed. "So before I came here, I was living in Venice. I met a woman on my way home from dinner one night. She was crying and her hair was a mess." He squeezed her hand, and Zara liked this soft, vulnerable version of the bad boy prince.

"So I took her back to my condo, and she told me

this big story about her boyfriend. We agreed that she'd stay with me for a couple of days, long enough to get him off her back." He sighed and leaned his head back against the seat. "But she stayed longer than that, and when I finally asked her to leave, she went straight to the press. Told them that we were married and that I'd broken up with her when she'd lost our baby."

Zara blinked, trying to make sense of all he'd said. She came up with, "Baby?"

"None of it was true." He looked at her again, his expression earnest and sincere. "I wasn't married. We didn't sleep together. There was no baby. She was just staying in another room in my place."

"Kind of like me," Zara said, recognizing the similarities there.

"Yeah, but you're not going to go to the press, are you?"

"No." She shook her head. She couldn't imagine a scenario where she'd go to the press and tell them anything about Noah.

He leaned forward, almost like he'd kiss her right then, and Zara's heart tumbled through her chest. But his lips touched her forehead, the gentlest of touches. "Thanks. So can we go surfing?"

She flipped the car into reverse. "Surfing. Yes. Let's go surfing."

SHE PUSHED INTO THE SURF SHOP FIRST, THE RAYS OF sunlight just starting to paint the sky behind her gold. "Morning, Rich," she said to the man standing a few feet away.

He turned toward her. "Zara." A smile filled his whole face, and he embraced her. Rich was probably ten years older than Zara, and his family had owned this surf shop for generations. They'd been friends since she was a little girl and her grandfather had brought her to the beach to learn to surf.

Her mother, of course, had not approved, but Zara had persisted in her pleadings to her grandfather, and they'd both won the argument.

"I haven't seen you in a while," he said, stepping back. His gaze flickered to Noah, who entered the shop behind her.

"Well, my show starts in less than a month," she said. "The rehearsals are so long." She hooked her thumb at Noah, mentally trying to come up with a way to introduce him. "This is...Holden. A friend I'm teaching to surf while he's here this summer."

The words tasted bitter in her mouth, but she kept her smile in place.

A friend.

She wanted to be a lot more than friends.

Holden.

Not even his real name.

While he's here this summer.

What would happen then?

The defenses around Zara's heart needed strengthening, because she did not want to wander the beach, looking for the broken pieces once Noah left Getaway Bay. And he was the prince of another country; there was no way he could stay.

Still, a nagging part of her brain wondered if he could. That maybe they just needed to talk about it, and make a plan, and everything would be fine.

Fine.

Another word that bounced around Zara's brain as Rich and Noah shook hands.

Nothing in her life had ever worked out to be just fine. She clawed and practiced for what she had, and sometimes she wished her life had been more like Noah's.

"So he needs a board," Zara said. "It'll probably have to be custom-made for his height and all that, but I'm wondering if you have something we can start with this morning."

"Sure," Rich said easily, the way he did everything. If he'd ever been upset or worried about something, she'd never seen it. "I've got something he can use until we get his made."

"Who makes the boards?" Noah asked, and Rich smiled at him.

"I do. Step over here, man, and let's get you measured." Rich worked around Noah, taking notes of his height, his arm span, his weight, all of it.

About twenty minutes later, Noah had paid for a

custom board that would be ready in seven to ten days, and he had a rental leaned up against his shoulder.

Zara's nerves pranced around inside her body, urging her to get down to the water and get this lesson over with. Then she could go to work, where the mental and physical requirements of her job would push any fantasies of Noah out of her mind.

They left the surf shop and faced the ocean. A handful of others were already in the water, and Zara set her sunglasses in place. "Let's go down this way a bit," she said, stepping to her right.

Noah came with her saying, "That was great. He was nice."

"Yeah, Rich is great."

"He reminds me of a friend I have in Triguard."

"Triguard?" she asked. "Is that the name of your country?"

"Yeah," he said. "Marco is easy-going too. Always brings me my favorite candy on my birthday. Doesn't seem to care that I'm a royal and he's a mailman."

Zara smiled at the nostalgia in Noah's voice. "When's the last time you saw him?"

"Last year, before I went to Venice."

"What's your favorite candy?" Probably something foreign she wouldn't be able to get.

"Peanut butter cups."

She almost tripped over her own feet, the loose sand half warm and half cold against her skin. "Really?"

He chuckled. "You thought it was going to be something weird, like Turkish delight." His eyes held that flirty, playful glint that had Zara's pulse in a tizzy.

"Yeah, sort of," she admitted, letting a smile touch her lips as her eyes dropped to his mouth. "I mean, peanut butter cups are so *normal*." As they stood there and watched one another, Zara realized that Noah was indeed normal. And that somehow made him more attractive.

"Yes, well, I'm human," he teased. "And for the record, Turkish delight *is* delicious if done right."

"Isn't that rose-flavored?" Zara made a face and started walking again.

"Yes, and the kind that is covered in powdered sugar and is super soft? It's divine."

"I'll take your word for it."

"Some people cover it in chocolate, but that ruins it for me."

"Anything covered in chocolate is better," she said.

He laughed then, a truly happy sound that filled the sky around them. Zara couldn't help joining in. Something sparked between them again, in this joyous moment with the sun just coming out to breathe life into the day.

Their eyes met, and he slung his arm around her shoulders. "Thanks for doing this," he murmured just before pressing his lips to her temple. "I know your days are long, and I appreciate it."

Zara gazed up at him, wondering if she could kiss him right there on the beach. There were other people around, but not many, and they were dozens of yards down the sand anyway. Her skin sizzled where his touched it, and the insanity of their situation somehow felt...sane.

She tipped up onto her toes and he bent down, brushing his lips against hers almost like he was seeking permission.

But she'd already given it, and in the next moment, he kissed her like he meant to, and everything in Zara turned into that super soft Turkish delight covered in powdered sugar.

She was aware of his rented board falling to the sand. Of both of his hands cradling her face and then moving into her hair. Of the way they moved together, fit together, breathed together.

Zara hadn't kissed anyone in a while, but wow. This was the best kiss she'd experienced in her life, and she felt as if Noah had just ruined her for any other kiss.

He pulled away first, and Zara drew in a deep breath. He kept his face in the hollow of her neck, his breath washing over her bare shoulder and making her shiver.

"So I guess we should probably figure out what steps we need to take," he whispered.

"Probably," Zara said, not wanting to complicate things with steps and talking and plans. She just wanted to exist in this moment with Noah for a while longer.

He kept her within the safety and comfort of his arms for a few more seconds, and when he inhaled as if to speak, she said, "But lets surf first, okay?"

She took a micro-step back and met his eye. He searched her face and finally nodded. "Okay."

Facing the water, the waves she loved, she said again, "Okay."

––––––––

THAT NIGHT, AFTER HER PRACTICE, ZARA TEXTED NOAH to see if he needed anything from town.

Just you came his response, and it filled her with warmth from head to toe.

"Ooh, who's Noah?" Suzie asked, splashing ice water on Zara's memories.

She flipped her phone over and said, "No one. Just some guy I'm working with."

"And he wants you." Suzie sat on the tiny bench and pulled on her running shoes. "So I guess you're not coming jogging with us."

"No." She glanced up at Jill who snapped a head-band around her forehead.

"So how are you getting your exercise in this week?" she asked. "Ian will be livid if you say you've laid by the pool for seven straight days."

"I'm surfing in the morning," Zara said, thinking of it on the spot. "So I run a bit there, and then paddle and swim and all that. It's quite strenuous."

Jill looked doubtful, but she shrugged and said, "Okay. Just don't want you to get in trouble."

"I won't." Zara had worked with Ian before, and she

knew what it took to earn his approval. She stood with a groan and rubbed her back. "See you guys tomorrow."

"Can't wait to hear about Noah," Suzie said with a dangerous glint in her eye. Zara just smiled and waved at her friends as they left. A pit opened in her gut at the fact that Suzie knew his real name. She probably should've put his pseudonym in her phone, but she hadn't. Suzie had already seen it.

Just you.

She shivered again, hoping tonight would include as much kissing as talking.

She showed up at the mansion with sushi and Chinese takeout, hoping Noah hadn't cooked. Even if he had, she could eat sweet and sour chicken for breakfast. After all, Chinese food was delicious any time of day.

Thankfully, the kitchen was devoid of food when she entered and set all her bags on the counter. "Noah?" she called, and a moment later, Boomer barked...from outside.

She turned that way and found the dog wagging his tail furiously from the other side of the French doors that led into the yard. She walked over to him and let him in, scrubbing him down with a smile and the words, "Where's Noah, huh?" The car he'd obviously driven at some point was still in the garage, but the house felt empty and Boomer's body was hot, as if he'd been outside for a while.

Concern rippled through her, but Zara pushed it back. Noah was a grown man. He could leave the mansion if he wanted to. The gate had been closed. The garage too. Still, she straightened and watched Boomer run over to his water bowl and begin to lap at a speed unknown to other dogs.

So, as she walked down the hall to make sure White-water was okay, she pulled out her phone and called Noah, hoping she wouldn't come off as too desperate or too worried.

He didn't answer, and she let her hand fall to her side. What should she do now? She filled the cat's food and water bowls, ready to go find Noah.

Her phone rang, and she practically threw it as she swung it wildly up to check who was calling. "Noah," she said once she got the call connected. "Where are you?"

"I fell asleep," he said, his voice still a bit on the slumbery side. "Are you home?"

"Yep. And I brought sushi and Chinese food."

"On my way down."

She hung up and went to meet him at the bottom of the steps. He swept her easily into his embrace, both of them laughing. "Hey, beautiful." He leaned down and kissed her, and it felt like the most natural action in the world.

"Hey," she said breathlessly when he pulled back.

"So," he said, taking hold of her hand and leading her into the kitchen. "I've been thinking."

"Oh, boy," she said. "Sounds dangerous." She unpacked the white Chinese containers and started popping them open.

"Ha ha." He took out the sushi and got out silverware and plates. "Anyway, I'd need to talk to my parents about leaving Triguard, but I don't see why they'd make me stay there."

Zara's eyebrows went up. "Are you serious?"

"I mean, I'm a prince, but I'm not going to be King. Ever. So why would I need to stay there?"

"I don't know," Zara said, her mind spinning a million different ways. "Family solidarity? United front? That type of thing."

"Yeah, they don't need me. I cause more problems than anything."

Zara watched him take a California roll and then scoop ham fried rice onto his plate. She heard the measure of regret and sadness in his voice. "I'm sure that's not true," she said.

"Trust me, it is." Noah met her eye briefly and went back to the food. "So anyway. I'm thinking of calling my mother tomorrow and talking to her."

Zara let a few seconds go by while she thought about how to phrase her next question. "Will she be...will you tell her about us?"

"Of course."

"And she'll be okay with you having another girlfriend only a week or two after your last one?"

That got him to look up, and when he met her gaze, she found sharp edges in his. "Katya wasn't my girlfriend. Ever."

"Did you kiss her?"

Noah's teeth clenched, and he said, "Yes."

"Ah, well, then she was your girlfriend."

"Is that a rule?"

Zara wanted to sigh and roll her eyes. "I realize different people have different benchmarks for such things," she said. "But to be clear, when I'm kissing a man, he's my boyfriend."

The fire in Noah's eyes changed from angry to something more like passionate. "Noted."

Zara took her food to her spot at the bar, thrilled when Noah sat right next to her instead of leaving an empty barstool there. "So you think you can move to Getaway Bay permanently?"

"I do."

And that was a huge step in the right direction. One that filled Zara with all kinds of emotions she didn't know how to sort through. Happiness, but also a bit of trepidation. Because if he moved here permanently, she didn't have an excuse for why they couldn't be together.

Chapter Twelve

Noah paced in his bedroom, the door closed and locked though Zara had gone to work an hour ago. He'd decided to start with Louisa, as his sister could tell him how their mother would react with near exactness.

But she wouldn't pick up the phone. So he hung up without leaving a message. She'd see he'd called, and she'd call him back when she was done with whatever obligation she was dealing with.

His stomach writhed as if he'd swallowed a nest of vipers for breakfast. As it was, he'd sipped a cup of coffee while Zara slathered peanut butter and Nutella on two slices of bread, grabbed a banana, and tucked a protein bar into her purse.

She'd flashed him a smile, kissed him quickly, and left through the garage door. He'd been sealed inside the mansion, but it didn't smother him as much as it had in the past.

His phone rang, and he jumped like he'd been caught on camera doing something naughty. "Hey, sis," he said when he answered. He sounded cool and confident, the way he'd been taught.

"Noah," she said, a brightness to her voice that felt genuine. "What's going on? You called three times."

"Did I?"

"In the span of five minutes. I was dealing with a member of Parliament, and I couldn't even get a text off."

Dealing with a member of Parliament. Noah didn't have to do that either. His mother actually warned him away from politics, citing his short fuse as the reason why. And he didn't even have that short of a fuse. But compared to her, Damien, and Louisa, Noah's temper was downright explosive.

"Sorry," he said. "I guess I'm a little anxious this morning."

"Why?" She drew the word out as if she were preparing herself for terrible news.

"So I'm at the mansion house in Getaway Bay," he said. "I've been here for a week or so." Had it really only been that long? And he'd already kissed Zara? A hint of embarrassment made his blood run hotter through his veins.

"And?" Louisa prompted, and he could just picture her all prim and proper as she chatted with him.

"And I'm thinking I'd like to just stay here." He drew in a deep breath. "Permanently." The word landed like a bomb between them, and Noah waited for his sister to say something. Anything.

"Have you spoken to Mom and Dad about that?" she asked, her voice quiet and downright diplomatic. He'd heard her speak like this before, and he didn't like that she was using the tone on him.

"Not yet," he said. "You're my sounding board."

"So Damien doesn't know either."

"No," he said. "Just you, and I'm just thinking out loud." He'd been doing more than that—in fact, his dreams and daydreams all featured him and Zara in the early-morning waves, surfing. Then doing something around the house. Or building a new children's wing in the library here on the island. Or chartering a jet and island-hopping for a few days. Or weeks. Whatever.

He didn't have a job, and he didn't need one. His inheritance was more than enough to buy a place and live on this Hawaiian island for a good long while. His whole life. Zara wouldn't have to work either, unless she wanted to.

He couldn't wait to see her swim, and he focused on the conversation. If he wanted a future with Zara, he needed to work some things out first.

"I don't know, Noah," his sister was saying. "No one in the royal family has ever left the island permanently."

"Is that true?" Noah asked. "What about that crazy uncle no one will talk about?"

"There's a reason no one talks about him," Louisa said.

"Well, maybe I'll be him," Noah said, though the thought of not being included in family texts and the royal events of the country stung him in a way he hadn't anticipated.

"Noah," Louisa said with plenty of reprimand in the name. "Why would you want to stay in Getaway Bay? To my recollection, you've never liked it all that much."

"That's because we never visit in the summer," he said, turning back to the window. "You should see this place right now. It's beautiful." And he didn't remember *not* liking Getaway Bay.

"And?" Louisa prompted. She really was the smartest of the siblings, and Noah should've anticipated that he'd have to tell her about Zara.

"And nothing," he said, his voice only the teensiest bit false. "Do you think Mother will veto it immediately?"

"Veto outright? No." Louisa paused for a moment. "But, Noah, you should expect to have an iron-clad argument in place. Just this morning, she mentioned she'd spoken to you and you'd be home soon."

"I didn't tell her that."

"You know how she is."

"Yeah." He sighed. "Does she have a parade all lined up?"

"Not yet." Louisa laughed and added, "But she did mention a new charity she wanted you to focus on once you return."

"I'm doing charity work here," he said. "I'm volunteering at a wedding planning place, and I'm donating to the synchronized swimming association here on the island." The last one had just popped into his head, but he seized onto it, determined to do it. No one had to know. His family had made plenty of anonymous donations.

"Mom said she didn't even know where you were."

"No, I didn't tell her."

"So I get the exclusive scoop." Louisa was the last person on Earth who would tell the press where he was. And honestly, he wasn't sure he cared anymore. If he was going to live here permanently, he couldn't take every trip down the bluff concealed under blankets in the backseat.

He chuckled. "Something like that, sis. So you think I need a better argument than it's pretty here in the summer."

"Definitely," she said. "And Noah? It better not be another woman."

He cringed at the word *another*, and he said, "Of course it isn't, Louisa," like such a thing was utterly ridiculous. They talked a bit longer about Damien's quick trip to the island, and if she was any closer to a firm date for her wedding. Then he hung up and returned to his position at the French doors, watching the ocean in the distance.

It better not be another woman.

Well, so what if it was?

He hadn't been in Venice for a woman, nor to run from a scandal. He'd simply been there on vacation. An extended vacation, sure, but not because he'd screwed up again.

Noah was tired of being the bad boy prince. He didn't want to return to his life in Triguard, even if it was somewhat fulfilling to volunteer and serve the people of his country. He wanted a more normal life, with a wife and kids and Boomer. He wanted to go to the beach in the summer, and carve pumpkins at Halloween, and establish his own family traditions for every other holiday.

And when he pictured himself doing those things, it was Zara at his side. So he lifted his phone again, this time calling his mother, no idea what he was going to say to her.

———

"YOU WANT ME TO MEET YOUR FAMILY?" NOAH STARED at Zara, her hair still damp from the pool.

She unpacked the grocery bags and started putting things in the fridge and cupboards as if she lived in this house. "We've been dating a few weeks now," she said. "My show opens next week. They'll see you there."

He'd told her about the tickets he'd found, and she'd simply shook her head, smiled, and kissed him like she was glad he was so resourceful.

He nodded and swallowed, suddenly so nervous. "And you don't think they'll be a huge roadblock?"

Zara shrugged, but Noah could read her expressions by now. And this one said yes, of course her family was going to be a major roadblock. He still hadn't gotten royal permission to relocate to Getaway Bay, and he'd made a dozen phone calls—two of them conference calls with the whole family—and the job still wasn't done.

His father simply didn't understand why Noah needed to live on a different island. Noah had steadfastly refused to tell them about Zara or the fact that she was house-sitting in the same mansion where he was currently living.

His mother would think that was a scandal, and she'd likely demand her money back from Zara and send someone from her security detail to retrieve Noah. So he hadn't gotten what he wanted yet, because he hadn't been able to give the right answers to his parents' questions.

But he didn't want to jeopardize Zara's job. He didn't want to lie. So he said nothing, and the frustration over the whole thing was starting to take its toll on him.

No, he didn't have official permission to leave Triguard, but he considered himself a permanent resident of Getaway Bay now. He and Zara had fallen into an easy and enjoyable routine. She drove him to Your Tidal Forever. He worked on whatever Hope needed him to do, and then he went to the beach, or hired a pro to teach him more about surfing. Whatever he wanted to pass the time until Zara finished with her rehearsals.

Then they grabbed dinner, went back to the privacy of the mansion, ate, and spent evenings together until one of them fell asleep.

It was almost always Zara, but Noah really didn't mind waking her and then leading her down the hall to her bedroom. He'd kiss her and leave her in the doorway before retreating to his own room on the second floor.

Nothing scandalous, no matter what his mother—or the press—might think should they ever find out how Noah and Zara spent their time.

They'd eaten at a different restaurant every night for the past few weeks, but never her family's. "So maybe we should stop by Indian House this week," he said casually, feeling anything but calm about the prospect.

Zara shook her head as she put crackers on a shelf. "Nope. That's not how it works. Meeting a boyfriend is a huge family affair. My mother will need at least a week's notice, and she'll do an entire Indian festival meal at the house."

Noah almost scoffed but caught himself in time. "What?"

"We've probably waited too long at this point," she said. "Schedules have to be rearranged so all my sisters can come. My aunts and uncles. Grandparents." She sighed as she cleared away the last of the recyclable bags and tucked them in a drawer in the island. "Maybe we should just show up at Indian House."

Noah got up and walked around the island, taking her easily into his arms. "I understand the formality of family things," he said, bending down to touch his forehead to hers. If there was anyone who understood the details that didn't matter, it was him.

"So you tell me what you want me to do. If you want the big meet-the-boyfriend affair, call your mom and set it up. If you don't, let's go to Indian House tomorrow night."

There was no reason they couldn't go tonight, other than the fact that Noah needed a little more time to gather his wits about him. He couldn't even imagine introducing her to his parents, and a slip of fear ran through him. He'd have to do that eventually, and he had no idea how it would go. After all, he couldn't even tell them she was the reason he wanted to relocate.

That's because of her job, he told himself. He knew she needed this job, and his mother would probably hop on her private jet and come to Getaway Bay to get her money back from Zara if she found out.

"Let me call her tonight," she said. "Maybe everyone can meet us for dinner tomorrow."

"I don't want you to think your family can't do their traditions," he said.

"I don't think that." She looked up at him, those honey-brown eyes smoldering at him.

"Good." He gave her a quick kiss and said, "Then let's go get tacos and watch the sun set at Lightning Point. Sound good?"

"Sounds amazing, but you have to bring way more blankets than last time. I got cold."

"I don't even know how that's possible, but okay."

"The wind was wicked," she said. "You were cold too; you just won't admit it."

No, Noah would not admit it. He simply shook his head and went to get another blanket out of the closet in the hall. He really liked spending time with Zara, and while they'd talked a lot over the past few weeks and gotten to know each other, they'd really only taken one step toward a lasting relationship—getting to know each other.

Him moving to the island was a huge step though, if he could get that to go through, and so was meeting her parents. He hoped it wouldn't take as much effort as getting permission to move here, but something told him he better be prepared for anything when it came to Zara's family.

Chapter Thirteen

Zara cuddled into Noah's side as the sun sank lower and lower into the ocean. The wind really whipped out here, and she was glad she'd grabbed a hoodie from her bedroom before they'd left. At least her hair wasn't flying out of control this time.

She'd decided to start with a text to Krisha, just to see what the family's plans were in the near future. That had turned into quite the texting marathon, and finally Zara shoved her phone in her pocket.

"Krisha knows something's afoot."

Noah burst out laughing, the sound joyful and his chest vibrating with the strength of it. "Afoot?" He snorted as he started laughing again, and that got Zara laughing too.

He kneaded her closer, and she thought back over the past few weeks in the mansion with him. She'd been terrified that Petra—his mother—would ask for her money back. But she'd never asked if Noah had met the house sitter or not. She'd never asked if Zara had run into Noah.

Of course, he hadn't told them about her yet. Every time she thought about that, her chest pinched a little. But he'd explained why, and she didn't want him to be dragged halfway around the world by royal security. Or give back her house-sitting fee.

He'd made every phone call in private, either while she was at work or behind his closed bedroom door. But she believed everything he reported to her. Apparently it was a much bigger deal for him to leave the country than either of them had thought.

The longer the drama dragged on, the more remote the possibility seemed that Noah would be able to move here. He'd said he'd start looking for a place of his own on the island, as his parents still visited Getaway Bay a couple of times a year. He thought that might sway them to allow him to relocate permanently.

To her knowledge, he had not looked for a place of his own, but she didn't care. If she thought the house was huge with him and Boomer there, she couldn't imagine how it would feel if they weren't.

"What else did she say?" Noah asked, bringing Zara back to this moment on the beach. This sunset. This breath. Zara spent so much time thinking about tomorrow—her next show. Her next paycheck. Her next boyfriend.

As she'd gotten to know Noah over the past month,

she'd realized that she wasn't living right now. And she wanted to change that.

"She said she thinks everyone will be at the restaurant tomorrow. As far as she knows, all the sisters are scheduled to work, and Mom and Dad eat there ninety-nine percent of the time."

"So we can go."

Zara drew in a deep breath, admiring the pink and purple among the gold and navy in the sky. "Yes," she said. "We can go tomorrow." She just wished she didn't feel like she was marching Noah up the side of a volcano and sacrificing him to the gods.

It's not that bad, she told herself. Her sisters would be nice, at least. Yes, some were more traditional than others, but they generally supported one another.

Noah ran his thumb up and down her arm, and she tuned in to the fact that he had some nervous energy of his own. "Are you worried about meeting them?" she asked.

"Five sisters and your parents in one go? Grandparents, aunts, uncles, the whole shebang?" He chuckled and added, "Nah. Should be easy. Nothing to it."

"You're such a liar," she said, giggling. "And look who's using outlandish words now. Shebang?"

Noah chuckled too, and Zara melted into the sound of his voice. Several moments passed, and then he said, "Of course I'm nervous about it, Zara," his voice soft and sober now.

She pushed away from his chest and looked at him. "Really? Why?"

"I don't know." He watched the horizon line, and Zara couldn't read the emotion in his eyes.

"You're a *prince*," she said. "If anyone should be nervous or worried about not meeting expectations, it should be me."

"I'm just a regular guy," he said, something he'd told her a few times over the past few weeks. Zara knew that. Well, deep down inside she knew he was just a normal man. But there was something kingly and royal about him she didn't think just anyone could learn.

"Should I go buy a new suit tomorrow?" he asked.

"Do you even have a suit here?" she asked.

"No."

"Then, yes," she said. "You should go buy a new suit tomorrow."

"Great," he said, seemingly glad for the opportunity. "At least I'll be able to get out of the house."

Zara giggled, but she knew the walls of the mansion trapped Noah from time to time. He didn't go volunteer at Your Tidal Forever every day, and while he rode in the front seat now, he wasn't exactly traipsing all over the island either.

She watched him, this handsome man that had come into her life unexpectedly. No, they had not gotten along in the beginning. But as she learned more about him and as she shared more about her, her heart had opened to the possibility of a real future with him.

"Thanks for doing that," she said, lifting up to kiss him. He received her willingly, and she sent a prayer up to whoever was listening that her family would accept Noah.

That seemed a bit far-fetched, so she amended her plea to just be, *Let them be kind to him,* and snuggled back into Noah's side to watch the night steal the last breath from the day.

———

THE FOLLOWING EVENING, ZARA TWISTED AND TURNED and looked at herself in the nicest dress she wore. She should probably be dressed in her nicest sari, but something about it felt false. Almost like she'd be manipulating her mother by wearing such traditional clothes.

She pulled on the hemline of the black fabric, sure it had always fallen a little lower than it currently was. She'd steamed it, and it fell down the lines of her body nicely, but would it be modest enough for her mother?

"I don't know why you care," she muttered to herself. Over the past decade, Zara had blazed her own path, unconcerned about her parents' feelings. But that wasn't entirely true, and she knew it. She did care about them, and how they felt, and her cultural traditions. She simply wanted to be her too, and her family still loved her.

She fluffed her hair one more time and deemed herself as good as she was going to get. Her heels clicked on the marble hallway as she made her way into the kitchen. Noah wasn't there, which meant he was probably twisting to look in a mirror and tugging at something to make it lay right.

She opened the fridge and promptly closed it again. She was starving, but they were eating at Indian House. With the way her stomach vibrated with nervous energy, she wasn't sure how much she'd actually be able to eat.

Noah's footsteps finally echoed off the steps, and he came into the kitchen a few seconds later. Zara froze, the breath in her lungs absolutely solidifying at the sight before her. If she'd thought he was good-looking before, she now had a new definition for the term.

He wore a suit the color of midnight, and it fit his frame perfectly. His shirt held the color of a pale winter sky, and his tie had pink, blue, and yellow checks among the black.

"How do I look?" he asked, as if he didn't know he was the best looking man on the planet.

Zara stared, sure this man was not her boyfriend. He seemed so far above her, and her self-confidence took a nose-dive.

"Zara?" he asked, stepping toward her. He smelled like musky cologne and soap, with a hint of mint from his toothpaste, and Zara wanted to breathe him in, hold him tight, and kiss him senseless.

He touched her elbow, unfreezing her, and she managed to say, "You look great," in a throaty voice. She cleared her throat and grabbed her purse from the kitchen counter. "Should we go?"

With a curious look on his face, he said, "Sure. Can I drive?"

She stalled in her flight toward the garage. "Do you remember how?"

"Ha ha," he said. "You think you're so funny."

"Well, you never drive, and you said even in Triguard, you'd get chauffeured around." She threw him a playful smile, hoping that would somehow elevate her to his status. But it was hopeless. A synchronized swimmer had no business being with a prince. "I'm just trying to make sure I don't die tonight."

Though she did risk her life with her car every time she got in it, as she still hadn't had a second of time to get it looked at or fixed. It kept starting, though, so that was something.

"You won't die." He put his hand on her back and guided her into the garage, grabbing the keys that had literally hung on the hook beside the door for a solid month.

She sank into his sports car—a rental he seemed to need to take up space in the garage—and adjusted her skirt while he settled behind the wheel. She buckled her seatbelt and cut him a quick look out of the corner of her eye.

He seemed utterly nonplussed, like he remembered where all the important pedals and switches were, and he backed out of the garage just fine.

Zara squinted into the bright sunlight and reached into her purse for her sunglasses. With someone else navigating the twisty roads, Zara simply enjoyed the sunshine and the way it glinted off the ocean in the distance.

Once they made it down to the town, she directed him down Main Street to Indian House. The parking lot was full, and every cell in her body rioted. Neither of them had said much on the drive down, and Zara took a few steadying breaths while Noah parked the car.

"Ready?" he asked, and while every stitch of him was in the perfect place, she could see the anxiety in his eyes. Somehow, it brought her comfort, and she nodded.

"Ready." She got out of the car, and Noah arrived on her side to close the door and link his fingers through hers.

"They're just people," he said as they walked toward the entrance. "We're people. It'll be fine."

"Is this your speech to yourself?" she asked.

"I mean, yeah," he said. "I haven't eaten all day, and I feel like I'm going to faint. My brain isn't working totally, so yeah. This is the best I've got right now."

"Why didn't you eat something?"

"Too nervous." He reached for the door and pulled it open to let out a blast of Indian music. Three or four couples waited in the area in front of the podium, and Abi looked up, a harried look on her face.

When she saw Zara, her smile erased the stress. "Zara," she said as if Zara could cure the crazy currently happening inside the restaurant. But it looked like a tour bus of Japanese travelers had arrived for dinner, and the whole place was packed.

Abi's eyes flickered to Noah. "Let me tell Mom and Dad you're here. They haven't taken dinner yet."

"Busy," Zara said, and Abi ran off. She turned back to Noah. "Maybe we should go. Try another night when things aren't so hectic here." She looked up at him, but he surveyed the restaurant, his dark eyes sharp and taking in every detail.

"Can't do it," he murmured, nodding toward something behind her. "Here come your parents now."

Zara spun around, her heart thrashing inside her chest. Sure enough, her mother and father were navigating through the restaurant toward them. Noah's hand slipped into hers and squeezed, and Zara tried to swallow.

Her throat stuck to itself, but she moved forward anyway. This was not the introduction she'd envisioned, and she hurried to press her hands together and say, "Namaste." Then she said, "Mother, we can reschedule."

"Nonsense, nonsense," her mom said, her eyes drifting past Zara to Noah. It wasn't like Zara could conceal him.

"You're terribly busy tonight," Zara said, tugging Noah to her side. "Really, we can do this another time."

"Nani and Dadi have a corner booth," her father said, nodding to Zara. "Come with."

"Come with," her mother said, gesturing with her hands. Always the hands.

Zara swallowed, a little moisture in her mouth now, and looked up at Noah.

"Let's go with, sweetheart," he said, barely loud enough for her to hear. And she really had no other choice. She went with.

She bowed to her grandparents, who watched Noah like he was a fascinating film. He was much taller than anyone else, and she finally stepped back and said, "This is Noah Wales, His Royal Highness, Prince of Triguard."

Her words hung in the air, and she could tell her family had not been expecting that. She'd asked Noah how he'd have been introduced in his country, and she'd written down the words and memorized them.

"It's just Noah," he said with a smile, reaching to shake her father's hand. He pulled it back quickly and instead pressed his palms together, his fingertips at exactly chin-level, and nodded. "Namaste. Nice to meet you, sir."

Her father bowed too, and said, "I'm Samir. Please sit down."

Noah bowed to her mother first, and he looked so odd performing the Indian customs she'd grown up with. At the same time, he seemed perfectly natural doing them, and she felt herself falling a little bit farther toward being in love with him.

Which seemed impossible. She'd only known him for a month, and there was still so much to learn about him. But what she did know, she liked.

"Sit," her mother said, and Zara slid into the booth, realizing that once her mother and father joined them, she and Noah would be sandwiched in the middle. No way out.

She kept her smile in place, and spoke to Dadi, her mother's father about her upcoming show.

"Your sisters can't join us tonight," her father said. "But we'll have a celebration at the house soon."

Zara exchanged a glance with Noah. "Oh, we don't need to do that. We're not engaged, Dad."

"Are you really a prince?" her father asked, and Zara's gaze whipped back to Noah's.

"Yes, sir," he said. "Triguard is a tiny island off the coast of Italy. My father's king there, and my older brother, Damien, is set to rule one day."

"So you will not rule," her mother said.

"No, ma'am," he said, taking Zara's hand on top of the table, right in front of everyone. She was surprised her skin didn't incinerate with the way everyone looked at their joined fingers. "Barring an accident where every member of my family is killed, I won't rule. In fact, I'm probably going to move to Getaway Bay permanently." He lifted his arm around Zara's shoulders and smiled at her.

Her mother's eyebrows went up, as did everyone else's at the table. "You can't move?" she asked.

"Not without permission." He reached for the glass of water in front of him and drank from it properly. He'd had some serious training in entertaining or etiquette, and Zara had never seen this side of him before.

He was charming, and dashing, and absolutely everything he needed to be to satisfy her parents. Auntie Tanvi appeared and swept her eyes around the group. "Family tray?" she asked, her eyes landing and staying on Zara.

Her father nodded and said, "Yes, Auntie," and Tanvi left. She wasn't really related to them, but she'd been a family friend for decades, and Zara had grown up calling her auntie. In most social situations, she'd expect her parents to ask Noah questions, but they just sat there, looking at him. She couldn't tell if they were star-struck or just nervous.

"So the show is coming along well," she said to get the conversation started. "We open in eight days."

No one said anything, and Zara felt this evening slipping away from her. Out of her control. And crashing fast. Her mind blanked, and she couldn't think of a single way to salvage this conversation, this meal, this relationship.

Chapter Fourteen

Noah had never been happier for his lessons about small talk, entertaining dignitaries, and appearing like he was having a grand old time when he really just wanted to go home.

He carried the conversation almost single-handedly with Zara's parents, who couldn't seem to do much more than ask him a question and then wait for the answers.

How old are you?

How many siblings do you have?

Do you have a job?

Zara finally said, "Dad, stop grilling him."

"I am not grilling him," her father said. "I am getting to know him. It's normal to ask questions."

"So you have no job?" her mom asked, as if she didn't believe him the first time.

"Well, I'm a prince," he said. "My job is to volunteer around the country and serve the people." With sudden realization, he realized why his father had been so resistant to letting Noah just slip away from Triguard.

No, they didn't need Noah to volunteer in the country's libraries. But if he left, what would the headlines say? There would be an assumed scandal, and the fact was, Noah's service did keep the royal family in a good light.

So maybe his part in Triguard wasn't completely useless. Every muscle in his body tensed, and he cut a glance in Zara's direction. She hadn't relaxed since they'd left the mansion, and Noah's helplessness had his mood sinking fast.

He was going to call his dad tomorrow, and now he dreaded the task. The only way he could fathom that his dad would let him leave Triguard was if he told him the truth. And that meant outing Zara as his girlfriend, not the house sitter.

"Noah," Zara said, half under her breath, nudging him at the same time.

"I'm sorry," he said smoothly. "What did you say?"

She looked at him with those beautiful eyes, which looked a bit shiny. Glassy. Full of tears? "My dad asked how you'll leave your country if your job is there."

Noah opened his mouth to speak, the perfect answer always right at the tip of his tongue. But he wasn't Damien or Louisa, and he simply sat there. He snapped his lips closed and smiled. "Well, people change jobs," he finally said.

Two of Zara's sisters, Myra and Sai, appeared, and

her mom and dad slid out of the booth to make room for them. Myra reached for the lamb and lentils and said, "So, Krisha says you're a prince."

Noah smiled, but he felt like he was about to crack. "That's right."

"Tell us about that." She looked genuinely interested, and thankfully, Zara came to life then, detailing the things he did, based on what he'd told her.

After they'd made it through meeting everyone and driving back up to the mansion in silence, Noah sat on the end of his bed, Boomer's head in his lap. "And it didn't go well," he told the dog after relaying a few other low points of the evening.

He heaved a sigh and finished taking off the suit. With a fresh T-shirt and a pair of gym shorts on, Noah collapsed back onto the bed. "I don't know, Boom. Maybe this is too hard." He stared up at the ceiling, realizing that he and Zara hadn't even cleared one roadblock on the highway toward a lasting relationship.

Her familial customs were so foreign to him. He hadn't expected that they'd fall down and worship him, but he had hoped for a smile at least. Her sisters seemed okay with the relationship, but Zara's parents had definitely been icy.

And he had no idea what to say to his father in the morning. As the minutes ticked by, Noah's mind went round and round, trying to find a solution that he was beginning to think simply didn't exist.

His phone rang before he'd gotten out of bed. He'd managed to fall asleep at some point in the night, and because he didn't have to go down to Your Tidal Forever today, he'd set no alarm.

He saw *the King calls* on the screen, and was immediately awake. He sat up and swiped open the call. "Hey, Dad," he said, his voice only slightly hoarse.

"Did I wake you?"

"I had a rough night."

"Not sleeping again?" Of course his father knew of Noah's insomnia. Just because he was King didn't mean he wasn't also a good father.

"I...." He paused, the words right there in the back of his throat. He felt like he was standing on the edge of a cliff, and the only way back down to safe ground was to jump.

"I met my girlfriend's family," he said, his voice soft but strong. "And it didn't go well."

Silence poured through the line, and it was amazing to Noah how thick and dense it could feel from halfway around the world.

"So this is why you want to leave Triguard." His father wasn't asking, and Noah would be surprised if he hadn't at least suspected that Noah had met someone in Getaway Bay.

"Yes," Noah said.

"Noah." He sounded tired, and Noah could just see

his father rubbing his forehead the way he did when he was trying to find the right thing to say. He never did it in public, but Noah had the privilege of seeing the king behind closed doors.

Noah said nothing. He had no defense for himself. His reputation as the bad boy prince didn't usually extend to women—until Katya. And then the press hadn't been all that surprised. He supposed his father wasn't either, and Noah didn't know what to do with how deeply his dad's disappointment cut him.

He'd once said, "I'm sorry I'm not Damien," to his father when they were arguing. His father had frozen, and all the fight had left his body.

"I don't want you to be Damien," his dad had said. "But you better figure out who you are and be that person."

Noah hadn't known what he meant at the time. He thought he knew who he was.

"Well, are you going to say anything else?" his dad asked. "Who is she?"

Noah pressed his eyes closed. He was not ashamed of Zara. He wasn't. But he also knew she was not the type of girl prince's brought home.

"Her name's Zara," he said. "She's a synchronized swimmer here on the island. She's...nice. She's *normal*, Dad."

"Mm," he said, making that humming noise that drove Noah up the wall. "Why didn't meeting her parents go well?"

"They're Indian," Noah said. "Very traditional. She's already broken ranks by not joining the family restaurant. It was just…awkward."

"But you still like her?"

"Of course," Noah said.

"And when can we meet Zara?"

"Oh, it's too early for that," Noah said with a chuckle. "We've only been seeing each other a few weeks."

"A few weeks?" The sharpness in his dad's voice sliced right through Noah's eardrums. "You only left Venice a few weeks ago."

"So it's been less than that. I don't know."

"I thought you were laying low."

"I was. I *am*." Noah hated how he felt like a child who'd done something wrong. Again. This was why he just wanted a normal life. No titles. No castles. No security detail. No crowns.

"Then how did you meet her?"

Noah hesitated again. "Promise you won't be angry?"

"Noah, you're thirty-one-years-old. Even if I was angry, what can I do?"

"Well, I thought Mom would send Ivan or Vince over here to get me."

"Oh, she's mentioned it."

Horror struck Noah right between the ribs. "She's not going to do that, is she?"

"I've managed to make that plan B or C," his dad said.

"What's plan A?"

"To treat you like you know what you're doing," his dad said, as if it was the most obvious plan of all.

"Dad, I have no idea what I'm doing." Noah didn't want to admit it, but he felt freer after the words left his mouth.

"Well, then, it's time to figure it out. Damien took a while too, but he's getting there. Your sister is days away from being engaged. Your mother wants you here for that Noah. And I do agree with her on that."

"Well, I can come for a party, sure," Noah said. "It's not like I'm never going to come to Triguard again. I just want…anonymity. And Getaway Bay is perfect for that."

"Mm."

Noah turned from the picturesque water beyond the glass in his bedroom. He paced over to the door and back. "Dad," he finally said.

"Louisa's engagement is on Wednesday," he said. "Your mother and I expect you here. We can discuss Zara and everything else then."

"Wednesday?" Noah echoed. "Dad, I don't know if I—"

"It's either you book your own ticket and be here by four p.m., or Ivan will come get you on Tuesday and escort you back."

"Dad, Zara's opening show is on Friday. I can't miss it."

"I don't see why you would."

But Noah nerves were vibrating. Even if he could fly

out early on Thursday morning, he wouldn't get back to Getaway Bay until Friday morning, what with the time difference. And a discussion with his mother and father had never gone less than an hour, and that was about which type of china the family should order for their heritage meal.

Something like Noah leaving the country and marrying a synchronized swimmer? That felt like an all-day session to him, and he'd most definitely miss Zara's show then.

"Noah, I'm inclined to grant your request, but I need something from you. A couple of things, actually. I need you here for Louisa's engagement announcement. And I need to know how you and Zara met."

Chapter Fifteen

Zara pushed herself out of the pool, the sound of Ian's bark coming easily through the water streaming off of her and through her swim cap. Her muscles trembled, and she was starving. They'd been practicing for ten hours, and she had a feeling no matter what happened, Ian would not be satisfied.

She stood on the deck, her chest heaving as she tried to make up for the oxygen she had deprived herself of while underwater. At least she wasn't in Ian's direct line of fire. But she knew she could do her kicks sharper, and she'd run into someone underwater on their last run. So she had some room for improvement too—and the show was only a week away.

Ian finally released them with, "Be here by eight tomorrow," which was an hour earlier than normal. Zara sighed, her stomach roaring at her for something to eat.

She stooped by her bag and pulled out a towel to wipe her eyes.

"Is he always this intense?"

She glanced over at the question, asked by James, one of the acrobats who did the high dives.

"Unfortunately, yes," she said with a weary smile.

James watched Ian's retreating back and then looked at Zara again. "A bunch of us are going to dinner if you want to come."

"Thanks," Zara said, a flash of missing hitting her. She usually did spend a lot of time with the cast of the shows she was in, exercising and getting meals. But since she'd met Noah, she'd driven straight back to the mansion to spend evenings with him.

"James," someone called, and he waved to them.

He turned back to her. "So are you coming?"

"Oh, she can't," Suzie said, appearing on Zara's other side and dropping her swim cap into her bag. "She's got a secret boyfriend up in this house on the bluffs." She was practically whispering by the end of her sentence.

Zara rolled her eyes as Suzie started giggling. "But I'd love to go to dinner."

James grinned and said, "All right. We're meeting out front in ten minutes. Everyone's invited." He walked away then, his broad shoulders rippling with muscles.

Zara tossed her towel into her bag. "Thanks for that." She lifted the bag, her shoulder groaning with the added weight.

"Well, it's true." Suzie followed her toward the locker room.

Zara wasn't sure if her friend was upset they hadn't hung out as much as they normally would have, or if she was just stating a fact. And Zara was too tired to try to figure it out. She'd eaten everything she'd brought from the mansion, and there was no way she was making it up the bluff without finding food first.

She opened her locker and saw her phone flashing with both green and blue lights. She was instantly twice as exhausted as she had been previously, but she reached for her phone with her free hand while she dropped her heavy swim bag to the ground.

She had texts from Noah, as well as two of her sisters. She had missed calls from Noah and someone named Petra. She frowned at that name, her slow, calorie-deprived mind taking a few extra moments to try to figure out who Petra was.

All at once, she remembered.

Noah's mother.

The woman who'd hired Zara to housesit the mansion on the bluff.

Her blood felt like ice in her veins, and her heart pumped harder and harder to keep her circulation going.

She sank onto the thin bench in front of the lockers and ignored Suzie when she asked what was the matter.

What was the matter?

Zara was going to lose her job, that was what the matter was. Not only that, she'd probably have to pay

Petra back. After all, the house-sitting gig was supposed to go through the beginning of September, and it was barely July.

She tapped on Petra's texts first. Sure enough, her words felt like cannons firing through Zara's system.

I just found out my son has been staying at the beach house, which means I obviously don't need a house sitter.

Zara decided to let the technicalities of what constituted a beach house slide by.

He claims there's been no impropriety, and that you are indeed his girlfriend. However, I don't need to pay someone to be my son's lover. Therefore, I would like you to be out of the house by tonight, and I will need two-thirds of the money back.

Zara's head felt like it weighed hundreds of pounds and she couldn't hold it up. Her neck ached, and her heartbeat wouldn't stop jumping around her chest.

There was no way she could be out of the house tonight. She had nowhere to go. And worse, his mother's words felt full of acid, and Zara feared she'd never please the woman now. The fact that she wanted to was ridiculous, but Noah was her boyfriend....

Not her lover.

Zara's fight and determination flew back into her body. So what if this woman was a queen? Zara had a contract with her, and she had been doing the job she'd agreed to.

Before arguing back with her, though, she swiped over to Noah's messages.

Zara, I just got off the phone with my father. I told him every-
thing. I'm so sorry.

Zara, call me when you go to lunch.

Zara, my mother is livid about the house-sitting. I'm trying to
talk to her. Don't do anything yet.

Zara, Zara, Zara.

He'd called twice too, and Zara's head hurt from all
the drama. All the swimming. So much hunger. She
slumped against the lockers, but all that did was make
her back hurt.

She'd known she and Noah were from different
worlds, and yet, she'd allowed herself to believe they
could build a bridge between them. One step at a time.
Wasn't that what Noah had said?

And she'd been foolish enough to believe him.

She shook her head and got to her feet. Petra wanted
her out of the house, so she'd get out of the house. She
hadn't spent any of the money she'd gotten from house-
sitting, so she'd just send some of it back.

Easy.

Done.

But she knew as she walked toward her car that
nothing about what was happening was easy. She knew,
because her heart was beating strangely. She knew,
because she didn't answer Noah's call when it came in.
She knew, because she didn't drive up the bluff to the
mansion the way she had been for weeks now.

Instead, she drove over to the Sweet Breeze Resort

and Spa and checked into a room. No, she couldn't really afford it, but all the performers in Ian's shows got half-price rooms at Sweet Breeze. So she splurged and ordered room service, showered while she waited, and wheeled the cart into her room wearing a fluffy, white robe once she was ready.

She ate, simply going through the motions her body needed to do to stay alive. Her mind whirred constantly, but she couldn't see a way out of the mess she and Noah had created. She shook her head at herself.

"What were you thinking?"

She pulled out her phone to text Petra an apology and that she was out of the house. She wasn't sure when she could go get her things—or Whitewater—but it didn't matter. She had her swim bag and her purse, and she could get her stuff out of storage as soon as she found a new apartment. Maybe Noah would feed White-water for her, but she didn't have the mental energy to ask him right now.

Another text from Noah had come before she could text his mother, and she hadn't heard her phone chime. *Where are you? Ian said practice ended over an hour ago.*

He'd called Ian?

A spark of anger ignited in Zara's blood. Of course, Noah had endless resources at his disposal—and she'd used her credit card at Sweet Breeze. So it was only a matter of time before he showed up here.

Instead of waiting for him to track her down, she sent him a text. *Sweet Breeze Resort, room 1215.*

Half an hour later, a knock sounded on the door, and Zara stared at it, trying to decide if she should open it and face Noah, or ignore him. Since she wasn't in junior high anymore, she crossed the room and unlatched the door before twisting the knob and opening it.

Sure enough, Noah stood there, his dark eyes blazing with all kinds of powerful emotions. "There you are. I've called you a bunch of times."

"Three times," she said, as if the number really mattered.

"Fine, three times." He stepped into her personal space, and she fell back to allow him entrance into the room. "Did you listen to my messages?"

"Nope." Zara let the heavy hotel door swing shut, the resulting *crash!* so loud she cringed.

"Have you texted or called my mother?"

"No, siree."

Noah turned and glared at her. "Zara, this is serious."

"I know this is serious," she snapped. "Why do you think I'm at this hotel I can't afford? Your mom told me to get out of the house by tonight. So I did. I've been off work for a couple of hours, and I was starving. So I showered and I ate, and I'm trying to figure out what to do." Her chest heaved, and tears pricked her eyes. She was so tired, and she just wanted the fun, easy, casual month she'd enjoyed with Noah to be her reality all the time.

His expression softened, and he said, "All right," in a voice made of marshmallows. "All right." He stepped into her and gathered her into his arms, holding her close to his heart while she worked to contain her emotions.

She did not want to cry in front of him. She would not.

"I spoke to my mother," he said. "I convinced her not to take the money back, because you have been taking care of the house. I do nothing there."

"You cook," Zara argued, because she could. Had he really asked his mother to let Zara keep the money?

"And I've moved out," he said. "So there's no reason you shouldn't be at the mansion, taking care of it according to the contract you signed with my mom. You'll earn your money, and you'll have a place to live." He pulled back and held her at arm's length. "Maybe now you can have your girlfriends up to the house for that pool party."

The way he looked at her, all soft smiles and crinkly eyes, and Zara became more confused than ever.

"You moved out?" The thought of staying in that huge house alone—which had once appealed to her greatly—now felt like a threat.

"Yeah. Boomer and I found a little cabin on the beach. It's nice, and he likes the ocean."

"You're such a liar." She could hear the fib in his voice. "Boomer does like the water, so the 'cabin' must not be nice."

"So it's missing a few amenities. I'll be fine."

"What kind of amenities?" Zara narrowed her eyes at him.

"I'll hardly be there anyway," he said instead of answering. "I'm flying to Triguard on Monday."

Alarm pulled through Zara. "You are? Why?"

"My sister is getting engaged on Wednesday, and I need to be there for the event. I'll be meeting with my parents on Tuesday night to talk about…everything."

Zara stepped out of his arms and searched for the bravery she needed to speak.

"What?" he asked when she couldn't quite find it.

"I think this might be too hard," she whispered.

"Zara," he said, his voice full of compassion but also argument. "It's fine. I've worked everything out."

And he likely had. He'd always been able to get what he wanted, even tickets to a sold-out show. But his parents had not granted him permission to leave Triguard permanently, and her parents had not appreciated that he was a prince. Apparently, nice Indian men were higher on the social ladder than royalty.

And she'd caused a rift in his family because of the house-sitting, and she felt dishonest though she *had* been taking care of the house the way Petra had asked her to.

"Did you tell your mom about my cat?" she asked.

"Of course not."

"You said everything."

"Well, I'd actually forgotten about Whitewater." He smiled at her gently. "Okay? Everything is going to be okay."

Zara didn't know what else to do, and she wanted to believe that Noah really could work everything out. So she nodded, let him draw her back into his arms, and bit back the idea of asking him if he at least had running water and a working sewer.

Chapter Sixteen

N oah knew there were different levels of comfort in a bed. Intellectually. But he'd never experienced it as first-hand as he did that first night in the beach cottage he'd found on a moment's notice.

Sure, he could've gotten one of the condos in the posh buildings near the new Ohana resort, but there wasn't anything available on the first floor. Noah didn't want to take an elevator ride every time Boomer needed to go out and take care of his business.

He'd searched online, and for being touristy, Getaway Bay didn't have a lot available for move-in immediately. Of course, it was the height of summer, and there would certainly be more opening up once autumn came.

He really hoped he'd still be on the island then, but his hopes for getting permission to leave Triguard permanently seemed like a distant dot on the distant horizon.

Like the sleep he was trying to get on this rock-hard

mattress. He finally pushed the flimsy blanket off and said, "Come on, Boomer. The hammock will be more comfortable than that bed."

He could call the furniture store and order the nicest thing they had, authorize them to come in whenever they could, even if he was back home.

Home.

He stared at the dark water, marveling at how it kept coming ashore no matter what. He also liked that it seemed mysterious and a bit sinister in the moonlight as opposed to how joyful and bright it was during the day.

Would Getaway Bay ever feel like home to him? Or would he be a perpetual vacationer here?

His day had been one of chaos. Dozens of texts and phone calls. Desperation all the way up his throat as he tried to find a way to appease his mother while keeping Zara employed. When he'd found out his mother had texted her *and* called her, demanding she move out of the mansion and return most of the money?

Noah hadn't felt that level of anger in a long, long time. Thankfully, he still had access to his bank account, and he'd found this beach house—er, shack—and said he'd already moved out of the mansion, that Zara was doing the job she'd been hired to do, and there was no reason that had to change.

His parents were not happy with him, and Noah wondered how old he'd have to be before they let him make adult decisions for himself. Because he was not letting Zara go without a fight.

As he watched the moonlight glint off the water, he had the sinking feeling that a fight was exactly what he would get when he touched down in Triguard. He'd booked his own ticket, choosing to go before the engagement announcement so he could return to Getaway Bay in time for Zara's show on Friday night.

He was absolutely not missing it.

Her words from earlier—*maybe this is too hard*—rotated around in his very alert mind. He hadn't liked the sound of them, and he'd promised her that everything would work out. But he honestly had no idea if it would or not.

Her parents hadn't liked him all that much, and the roadblocks they faced seemed insurmountable. He collapsed into the hammock, glad he was right about one thing. It was infinitely more comfortable than that blasted bed.

―――――

SUNDAY NIGHT, HE DROVE TO THE AIRPORT, READY FOR HIS trip to Triguard. It would take a day and a half to get there, and he was already annoyed. He landed in Newark sometime near morning, and had half a mind to wander around the state of New Jersey as if he were a regular man. Maybe ride the subway or visit a park. Maybe carry a briefcase, like he had a job to get to like everyone else.

In the end, he found a hotel that would let him check into a room that hadn't been used the previous night, and he slept for most of his eighteen-hour layover. The bed

The sun shone brightly in Triguard when he landed, which totally didn't reflect his mood. Exhaustion weighed him down, and he just wanted to crawl into bed and sleep for a while. Though he'd flown first class, his legs didn't fold right on an airplane, and he was in no mood for the press—or for his family for that matter.

But word had obviously gotten out that he'd be arriving today, because the reporters were five deep as he walked out of the airport. His father had decreed they could not go inside, and there was a special, roped-off area for them.

Noah had never been happier for sunglasses, as he was sure if the photographers caught sight of his eyes, they'd have a dozen speculations as to why he looked so thrashed. As it was, he grinned and lifted his hand in a royal wave, as if he was so incredibly happy to be back in his home country.

He took a deep breath, his grin stuck in place, and a strong pull of happiness did move through him at being home. After all, there was nothing like his mother's hug, and he was suddenly anxious to get on his way toward the castle.

But he knew he had some major public relations work to do, so he signed whatever someone put in front of him, noticing that there were several children with books they wanted him to scrawl his name in.

He took the most time with them, asking, "Have you read this one?"

"Yes," the little boy said.

Noah flipped it over and looked at the front cover. "Oh, I love this one." He grinned at the boy, who couldn't be older than ten. "The ending is a little sad, don't you think?"

He nodded, his eyes wide. His mother kept a grip on his shoulder like Noah might somehow infect him with some sort of bad boy disease if she let her son get too closer. Noah tousled the boy's hair, and said, "Well, keep reading, bud. It's the best way to travel."

He straightened and smiled at the mom, who grinned right back at him. He repeated this process until everyone had been satisfied. The press had taken hundreds of pictures, and once the last person had been taken care of, a reporter yelled, "Where have you been, Prince Noah?"

Prince Noah.

He hadn't been called that for a long time.

"Overseas," he said. "Great for the psyche."

"Are you home for good?" someone asked at the same time someone else called, "Are the rumors about Princess Louisa true?"

Noah waved and hitched his bag higher on his shoulder. "I've been gone for months. I'm sure I don't know what's going on with my sister." He glanced around for his ride, sure his father had arranged something for him.

After all, Noah had passed along his flight info, which someone had obviously "leaked" to the media.

He'd been standing outside talking to people for about twenty minutes now, and as he glanced down the busy street, he saw the long limousine with the royal flags. He stepped right over to the curb and lifted his hand as if the driver wouldn't know where he was.

Sure enough, Luc eased to a stop with the back door only inches from Noah's hand, but he didn't open the door. He never did. He waited for Luc to do it. After all, they paid the man an exorbitant amount of money to drive the limousine and open doors.

He came around and said, "Good afternoon, Prince Noah. So good to see you."

Noah's heart swelled, and he said, "Good to see you too, Luc." And it really was. The servants had never judged Noah, and he'd never been so appreciative of that fact as he was right now. Luc reached for the door handle, and Noah edged to the side, almost desperate to get in the car, get behind those tinted windows, get some relief from this public appearance stuff he wasn't so good at.

But Luc didn't allow him into the car. He stood back as Noah's father, the King himself, unfolded his tall frame from the car. He buttoned his suit coat and looked at the press. He lifted one hand and smiled the same way Noah had before turning to his son.

So many things were said in those few seconds. So much communicated with the meeting of eyes and a few moments of time. Noah's emotions swelled and roared, and he knew his father loved him. Screw ups and all.

His dad took the couple of steps to Noah and embraced him, sending the reporters into a complete tizzy. "Welcome home, son," he said, his voice soft and sincere, and Noah held onto him like his life depended on it.

It was as if thirty-one years of emotions bubbled to the surface all at once. Noah had kept everything bottled up, only showing what he couldn't control in rare instances. He'd long thought his brother and sister were simply better at everything, but really, they were better at blowing off steam behind closed doors, while Noah sometimes erupted when there were cameras around.

He stepped back as his father released him and turned back to the crowd. "Thank you all for respecting the crown," he said. "And don't forget. We have a royal announcement tomorrow evening, at six p.m." With that, he turned toward Luc, nodded, and slid gracefully into the back of the limo.

Noah followed him, ignoring the shouted questions from the media. Inside the car, he found his mother and Damien, and surprise rolled through him that they hadn't gotten out of the vehicle.

"Mom," he said, accepting her side hug, which wasn't nearly as good as the full thing. He glanced at his brother, who wore a completely unreadable look. "What's going on? Where's Louisa?" Might as well have made it a family reunion in the back of the limo, though it was bad enough the King and his heir were in the same car.

Something was really going down, and nerves ran through Noah.

"She's busy preparing for the engagement announcement," his mother said.

"Why didn't you guys get out?"

"Clara said it would be more powerful to have your father welcome you home." His mother flicked something invisible off her skirt. "She said I always forgive you, and you needed to be seen with the King as he welcomed you back with open arms."

Noah met his father's eye again. "And am I welcomed back with open arms?"

"Of course," his dad said, and Noah nodded. Their conversations these past few weeks had been civil. Personal. Familial. Noah had never felt like he didn't belong in his own family—not the way Zara did. He just felt…stifled by the royalty of it.

"What else did Clara say I need to do?" he asked, thinking their press secretary should've come along for the ride too.

"She's lined up a speaking opportunity for you," his mother said, exchanging a glance with Damien.

"Mother, I'm not going to be here long enough for a speaking opportunity." His flight left on Thursday at noon, and with the day and a half trip home, and the eleven-hour time difference, he'd have exactly an hour to spare before Zara made her first dive into the water.

He was not missing it.

His mom said nothing, and Noah looked at Damien too. "What's going on?"

Time seemed to slow as the car continued to move, but no one spoke. Only his mother looked uncomfortable, and Noah realized Damien really was ready to take the throne.

"We need you to stay for a few weeks," he finally said.

"A few weeks?" Noah practically yelled, heat shooting from his toes to his brain. "No." He shook his head now. "I can't do that. I can't."

"We checked on Zara's show, dear," his mother said like he was being petulant on purpose. "It runs all summer. You can see it when you return."

"No, I can't," he said. "It's sold out, and I had to beg, borrow, and practically turn over my inheritance to get the tickets I did." He couldn't miss opening night. It meant a lot to Zara, and he had to be there.

"We're sorry," his mother said, and Noah wanted to rage at her. Sorry? In that moment, he didn't understand his parents or his brother. Couldn't they understand he wanted something different for his life?

"We'd like Zara to come here," his father said, and Noah's gaze shot to him.

"She's working, Dad. She can't just leave the show."

"Of course." He looked out the window.

"Well, Louisa needs an escort around the island as she celebrates with the people, and Clara thought you'd be the best man for the job. It'll repair your reputation and allow you the opportunity to leave Triguard as you wish."

"Why can't Eric escort her?"

"He'll be with you, yes," Damien said. "But it's improper for them to travel alone, and they need an entourage."

Noah scoffed. Of course Louisa and Eric wouldn't be traveling alone. They'd likely have two security guards each, with an additional four undercover, following from a distance.

"This is ridiculous," he said. He wondered what his parents would do if he snuck out of the castle and tried to board the plane on Thursday the way his original itinerary had planned for him to do.

Desperation clogged his throat, and he wanted to text Zara right now and tell her how insane his family was being. But it was two o'clock in the morning there, and he didn't want her to know about any speedbumps.

Then she'd say their relationship was too hard, and when he got back to Getaway Bay—*if* he ever did—she wouldn't be his to kiss anymore.

"I have a plane ticket," he said.

"We'll exchange it," Damien said easily, as if he himself knew how to do such things.

"Louisa needs you, dear," his mom said, and Noah shook his head.

"No, she doesn't."

"No," his father said. "She doesn't. But Noah, you have things to explain to us about Venice, and a reputation with your countrymen to fix because of it. Then we want to know everything about Zara, and how you two met and what's been happening between you. And then, *if* you behave while on this engagement tour, then I'll consider letting you leave Triguard."

Noah heard the threat in his father's voice, definitely heard the emphasis on the word *if*, and absolutely saw the blazing fire in his dad's eyes.

He leaned back against the seat, wishing with everything inside him that he'd never come home. Because it felt like now that he was back on the tiny island where he'd been born and raised, he would never be leaving it again.

Chapter Seventeen

Zara shook out her hands, her performance swimming suit on, along with her cap and her goggles. Her nerves zipped through her with the crackling speed of electricity, and she hoped her parents hadn't had too hard of a time parking.

They didn't like coming down to the beach, but the venue was partly outdoors, and there wasn't a lot of parking. If they'd park over by Your Tidal Forever, there'd be a shuttle, but her dad complained about those too.

Hopefully one of her grandparents had just dropped them off.

Zara couldn't believe her thoughts were consumed with her parents and their parking woes. At least they were here. Noah had texted a few times and called once to say that he wouldn't be making it to the show.

Her disappointment still tasted bitter on the back of her tongue, coated her throat as she tried to swallow.

"You ready?" Suzie asked, wearing the same swimming suit as Zara.

"Yes," she said, pushing her parents and Noah and everything out of her mind. She needed to focus and put on the performance of her life. People had paid a lot of money to come see this show, and she'd rehearsed for hundreds if not thousands of hours to give them something to talk about.

"You're up," Suzie said, and Zara pushed out of the locker room and made her way into the pool, securing her nose clips as she went. She dove down to the platform and grabbed on to the handle there. She held her breath and fluttered her feet slightly.

The platform jerked, and she went with it, her feet slamming into it as it moved up, up, up and out of the water. It rose about ten feet, and then a man named Beni joined her, his smile as wide as hers.

Then the platform ascended again, the acrobats and swimmers around them climbing and flipping and creating beautiful, three-dimensional art with their positions.

The music crescendoed, and right at the height of it, she and Beni pushed off and leapt into the air. She flipped and twisted, straightening out about halfway toward the water. She entered the pool cleanly, a definite slap of water against her senses, but she could still hear the applause.

Or maybe she was hallucinating. She wasn't sure.

But when she pushed herself out of the pool and waved at the crowd, they definitely cheered louder for her, the female high-diver that had started the show with a bang.

She slipped back into the water and got in formation with the other girls, their synchronized movements so familiar and comforting that Zara forgot about the empty house she had to go home to, the lecture she'd probably get from her mother about the high cut of her swimming suit, and the fact that Noah was probably never going to get permission to leave Triguard.

Okay, so that last one didn't get completely forgotten, but at least it took up space in the very back of Zara's mind, leaving her room to focus on the show.

After the show ended, Zara wrapped herself in a robe and went to see her family.

"You were wonderful, Zara," her mother said, drawing her into a hug. "Just wonderful." She kissed both of Zara's cheeks and beamed at her. "How you wear that swimming suit, I don't know, but that dive. Oh." She put her palm over her heart and looked at her husband. "Wasn't she wonderful?"

"So good," he said. "Just so good." He embraced her too and all of Zara's sisters came forward. She appreciated their support, and her emotions swirled and made her choke up a little. Thankfully, she didn't cry, and after all the congratulations and all the hugs, she went back into the locker room to get packed up.

Her body hurt, and all she wanted to do was go home. In that moment, under the bright fluorescent lights in the locker room, she realized she didn't have a home.

Not really.

The mansion on the bluff wasn't hers. She'd given up her apartment.

"Coming to dinner with us?" Jill asked, pulling her swim cap off.

"Yes," Zara said immediately. The cast usually went out together after shows, and she was thrilled she could prolong the solitary drive up to the bluffs. "I'm starved."

Jill laughed and started changing. She and Suzie accepted Zara right back into the group as if she hadn't abandoned them for the past month while she and Noah dated. As she walked with them out to Suzie's car, she couldn't help checking her phone.

Noah knew what day it was, and she expected to see a text from him. A quick note of luck. Something.

Her screen was blank.

Triguard was eleven hours ahead of Getaway Bay, and surely he was out of bed by now. In fact, she'd never known him to sleep much past five o'clock in the morning.

But he hadn't texted, and Zara's heart withered a little as she got in the backseat of Suzie's sedan. She shoved her phone in her pocket when Suzie said, "So, I'm seeing this guy named Ryan...."

ZARA DIDN'T HEAR FROM NOAH IN THE MORNING, NOR did he text or call on opening weekend at all. She was beginning to think he'd fallen off the face of the Earth, or that he'd been a mirage on this island when she'd needed someone the most. Or that he'd been lying to her this whole time about who he was.

So Monday morning, she sat down with her laptop at the kitchen counter where she'd eaten his cooking dozens of times. She pulled up a search window and put his name in. The results exploded down the screen, and he definitely existed.

Relief sighed through her.

Not only did he exist, but he was also a prince. Double sigh.

And if the pictures and headlines could be believed, he was currently on an engagement tour with his sister Louisa, and her fiancé Eric.

Exactly as he'd told her he would be. He hadn't mentioned that he would be completely unavailable or that he'd forget about her the moment he stepped foot back on his home island country of Triguard.

Zara tried to push away the negative feelings. She slammed her laptop closed with a little too much force, her frustration at his complete silence digging into her in the most uncomfortable way. But he'd known how hard she'd been training for this show, and he'd seemed genuinely upset that he wouldn't be able to use his tickets.

With nothing to do until later that afternoon, Zara suited up and wandered out to the pool. She'd thought this summer would be one of relaxation with fruity drinks, and it hadn't been that way very often.

But today...today, she was going to spend the morning poolside, with that strawberry mango smoothie and the hot Hawaiian sun beating down on her.

And tonight? Tonight, she was inviting all the cast members to come to the mansion for a midnight pool party. Thinking fast, she swiped open the app on her phone and started tapping to order a few groceries. Soda and chips, salsa and dips, sub sandwiches, and a veggie platter should do the trick.

After all, she couldn't spend all her free time pining away after Noah. The pictures she'd glimpsed on the Internet were enough to know he certainly wasn't shut away in a castle tower, moping about.

No, he'd been wearing expensive suits, and waving to the crowd, and signing autographs. She glanced at her phone. Maybe she could just call him. It would be evening in Triguard, and maybe he could talk for a few minutes. She went back inside and distracted herself by making the smoothie she wanted. But back by the pool, her phone taunted her.

In the end, she sent off a quick text that said, *Opening weekend went great! Hope you're having fun on the tour.*

He didn't answer, and Zara smoothed sunscreen over

her exposed skin, knowing the last thing she needed was a sunburn. An hour later, after she woke from her catnap, she texted Suzie about the pool party that night, opened the door when the grocery delivery guy arrived, and checked her phone obsessively.

Noah still had not answered, and her frustrations were starting to morph into worries. Maybe something had happened to him. Maybe he'd lost his phone. Maybe it had been damaged from a stampeding herd of women, chasing after the handsome, eligible prince-bachelor.

Zara disliked the poisonous thoughts in her mind, but it sure seemed as if Noah had forgotten about her already. And as much as she wished that idea didn't sting her to the core, the fact was that it did.

As she went through her swim bag one last time to make sure she had everything for that night's performance, her phone finally chimed.

The message said it was from Noah, and Zara's heart tapdanced inside her chest.

I am having fun on the tour.

Zara stared at the words, trying to make sense of them, when another text came in. *Prince Noah seems to be as well.*

Prince Noah. Zara's fingers tingled and she felt a little removed from her body as the realization that someone else had Noah's phone hit her. *Who is this?* she typed out and sent.

Katya.

Zara stared at the single word. No last name, as if Katya was as famous as someone like Madonna or Cher.

What in the world was Noah doing on his sister's engagement tour with the woman who'd ruined his reputation?

Had he been lying to her this whole time?

She checked the time—she was about to be late—and saw that it was almost two-thirty. So it was one-thirty in the morning in Triguard. And Katya had Noah's phone.

Zara's stomach twisted and turned over, making her feel like she was about to throw up. She didn't want to keep talking to Katya, but she had no guarantee that Noah would ever get his phone back.

She stuffed her phone in her back pocket, shouldered her bag, and stormed out of the house. She had a show to do. A party to put on. And sleep to get.

Then she'd figure out what was going on with Noah and Katya.

Chapter Eighteen

N oah pressed his back into the door of the villa, his fingers fumbling to make sure the lock had engaged. He wouldn't put it past Katya to come barging in without knocking, as she'd done it twice on this tour already.

His head pounded with thoughts of Zara and what she must think of him. He had to figure out how to get in touch with her. He knew what he needed to do; he just didn't want to ask his mother for Zara's phone number during the tour. He didn't want to jeopardize his chances of getting permission to leave his country for good.

At the same time, he wondered why he needed permission at all. He'd been gone for several months before, and why couldn't he just relocate and return to Triguard for visits? But he knew that princes didn't always get what they wanted, especially those who wouldn't rule.

Maybe he could ask Louisa to ask their mother for Zara's number.

Always back to Zara.

But Noah felt like he was one breath away from suffocating without being able to contact her. Everything had happened so quickly, and he could barely make sense of it even in quiet moments.

"Ambushed," he muttered to himself as he pushed away from the door. His family had ambushed him with Katya's presence and subsequent announcement that she would be accompanying him on the engagement tour.

Three weeks with the woman who'd lied about him, caused him to flee Venice, and didn't even appear remorseful about any of it. Oh, no. His mother had been busy buying her dresses and getting her hair fixed so Katya could be presented as respectable. So she could hang on his arm and they could pretend to be together.

"Just for a few weeks," his mother had said, looking at Clara. The public relations director had then launched into the insane plan to restore Noah's reputation, at which point he and Katya would have a quiet break-up, and if he'd behaved and played his part well, he might get what he wanted most—Zara and a normal life in Getaway Bay.

He might have been able to go along with the plan better had he been able to communicate with Zara in any way. But his phone had been "accidentally" dropped into the koi pool in his mother's personal suite, and he'd been presented with a new one.

A new one without any contacts in it, and he didn't memorize phone numbers. He'd messaged Zara through the one social media app he'd found her on, but she hadn't responded. She didn't look terribly active there, as her last post was four months old. With every minute and hour that passed, Noah's hope leaked away.

Knocking sounded on his door, and he jumped like a skittish cat. Couldn't he get five minutes of peace?

"Who is it?" he asked through the solid wood.

"Louisa," his sister said. "Hurry up and let me in."

Noah did exactly that, and she darted into the room. He closed the door swiftly behind her and asked, "Who are you running from?"

She patted her hair, smoothing her royal persona back into place along with the errant strands. "Katya."

"Oh, so that makes two of us." He gave her a dark glare and went back into the kitchen. There'd be no alcohol here, and even if there was, Noah wouldn't consume it. He knew better than to drink and try to impress people and reporters at the same time.

He did need an escape though, and the fact that Louisa did too spoke volumes.

"We're at the very beginning of this tour," he said. "Are we going to survive?" He opened the fridge and found soda and water. "Want something to drink?"

"Water, please."

He handed his sister a chilled bottle and took one for himself too. "Why are you doing this tour?"

"Mother thought it would be good for my image,"

she said. "Damien's not married, and he doesn't have many prospects at the moment. It's quite…untraditional."

"Well, maybe some of our traditions should be changed."

"Noah," Louisa said reprovingly.

"What will happen when you produce an heir first?" he asked, lifting his eyebrows. "I mean, come on, Louisa. Does it really matter if you tour for weeks?" He shook his head as he uncapped his bottle.

"Damien will be King," she said. "And his first heir will be next in line, no matter how many children I have first."

"Exactly," Noah said. "So why does it matter if you tour around, shaking hands and smiling for the camera? It doesn't make a bit of difference."

"It does in public perception," she said.

Noah grunted and drank. After swallowing, he said, "And public perception is all that matters."

Louisa opened her mouth, probably to argue, but more knocking came on the door. Noah knew this rap, and he rolled his eyes. "Katya."

"She really is an interesting woman," Louisa said.

"She really was in trouble that night in Venice," Noah said, wishing it didn't come out so defensively.

"I know." Louisa put her hand on Noah's arm, drawing his attention from the closed door. "Father looked her up. Everything about her. Interviewed her three times. We believe you, Noah. It's just—"

"About public perception," they said together.

"I know," Noah added, a sigh of exhaustion passing through his whole body. "I don't know if I can do this for two more weeks."

"You have to." She straightened and tossed her long, dark hair over her shoulder. "I'll deal with her tonight."

"Thank you," Noah murmured. "Louisa?"

She turned back to him, and the powerful connection of siblings flowed between them. He saw her as a small girl who he used to follow around. She'd pour tea for her animals, and she only ever let him bring one "guest" to the parties—a ratty stuffed elephant he'd gotten from their excursion to Africa when he was four years old.

"Could you maybe get Zara's number for me? Or get in touch with her and let her know what's going on?"

Sadness crossed his sister's face. "I can't, Noah."

"Why not?"

"Because any little leak to the press about how this isn't real could be disastrous for us."

"And you trust Katya to keep her mouth shut?" Because Noah didn't. The woman had already lied and spread rumors once.

"Father does," she said. "So I must."

"So no Zara."

"Not for a few more weeks," Louisa said. "I'm so sorry, Noah. It's obvious you care for her."

Noah nodded, his jaw tight, his teeth clenched, his heart struggling to beat. He wasn't sure Zara would be overly excited to hear from him in a few weeks. In fact, he was quite sure she'd break up with him long before then.

"If she loves you as much as you love her, she'll understand." Louisa ducked her chin and turned back to the door. Noah moved out of sight as she opened the door and said, "Katya, why don't we take dinner in my suite tonight?"

The door closed behind them, and Noah hurried across the room to lock it again.

If she loves you as much as you love her.

Noah wasn't in love with Zara. Was he?

He shook his head, his stomach grumbling for something with more calories than water. No, he wasn't in love with Zara—unless she was in love with him. Could she be in love with him?

The confusing thoughts went round and round, and Noah wanted nothing more than to talk to her. Hear her voice. Assure her that nothing she saw online was true and that he was doing everything he could to return to her and Getaway Bay as fast as possible, for as long as possible.

But he couldn't even text her, and Noah had never been so frustrated.

———

A WEEK LATER, NOAH'S IRRITATION ONCE AGAIN ROSE TO a level he'd never known. He kept a tight grip on Katya's hand, his plastic smile cemented in place. But he was livid and about to blow. He wished Louisa and Eric would hurry up and finish so he could get away from this insufferable woman, get out of this excruciatingly hot suit, and somehow find relief.

He'd never been overly religious, but he prayed now, harder than he ever had.

Because Katya had kissed him. Right in front of the reporters, as if they were so madly in love and couldn't wait to be on their own engagement tour. In fact, she may have said those words. Noah's anger roared through him, blocking out other sounds.

The sun beat down. The wind died. Katya's hand in his tried to wiggle away but he squeezed it tighter. And still Louisa talked and nodded.

Finally, finally, she turned and saw him. Alarm crossed her face, and Noah's hope diminished a little more. If she could see his discomfort and annoyance so easily, so could everyone else.

She wrapped up her conversation and waved to the crowd one final time before turning and walking past him and Katya, Eric's hand on the small of her back. Once they were safely inside the library, where Noah himself would be speaking to a group of teens and their parents, Louisa asked, "Will you excuse us?"

The security detail fell back, leaving the four of them to go on alone. Louisa turned toward the door where a woman wearing a name badge stood, and she said, "Noah and I need a moment." She was all smiles and perfection as Noah went past her into the room.

Once the door was closed, he finally released the breath he hadn't realized he'd been holding. "I can't do it," he said, a moan following. "Did you see what she did out there?"

"No, what happened?"

"She kissed me." He braced his hands against a table, trying to get enough air now. "Louisa, this isn't helping. This is only going to make me look worse when we break up." *And what about Zara?* his mind wailed.

Louisa stepped back to the door and opened it a few inches. "Eric, darling, could I have my phone please?"

"What's going on?" he asked, handing it to her.

"Come in a moment." Louisa backed up to let her fiancé in. Noah liked the man. He was charming and good-looking too. A duke from a neighboring island nation. And he adored Louisa and she him, and in Noah's mind, that was all that mattered.

"Oh, no, I just need Eric. Thanks, Katya. We'll only be a moment." Louisa closed the door, dropping her princess politeness as soon as the click sounded. She began tapping and swiping on her phone, and then she gasped.

Her eyes lifted and met Noah's, and she turned the phone to him so he could see what she'd found. Pictures.

Oh, how he hated pictures. And cameras. And anyone who wielded a camera.

"See?" he said. "My name's going to be in even more headlines because of this. And not good ones." He paced away from his sister and her fiancé. "Why did anyone think involving this woman was a good idea? I said it wasn't from the very first mention of her." He shook his head, his teeth grinding together again. It was a miracle he had any enamel left.

"I'm sending it to Dad," she said.

"Who cares?" Noah asked bitterly. "The pictures are already out there." He stared out the window, feeling more lost and alone than ever. Even when he stood at the glass door in the mansion in Getaway Bay, he hadn't felt this low.

Eric stepped next to him. "I got Zara's number," the man said, so quietly that it took several seconds for Noah's brain to register that Eric had spoken.

"What?" Noah looked at Eric, who steadfastly gazed out the window.

"Sh," he said, his mouth not moving. "Don't look at me."

Noah returned his attention to the glinting sunshine outside.

"Hand me your phone," Eric said. "Carefully now."

Noah moved centimeter by centimeter, finally getting his phone onto the windowsill in front of him and Eric. He wanted to look over his shoulder at Louisa, but he didn't dare. He could hear her sighing, and her phone kept chiming with each message that came in.

Painfully slow, Eric picked up Noah's phone, and then he moved quickly. How he could swipe and tap without truly looking down was a skill Noah needed to start working on. But only seconds later, Noah's phone was back on the windowsill, and Eric had fallen a step or two away

"Don't tell Louisa," he said in that same low voice before turning back to her. "What's your father saying?"

"He doesn't know what to do either. He's called for Clara."

"That woman won't know what to do," Noah said, leaving his phone where it sat. "Katya is a liability. A loose cannon. No one can predict what she'll do. And now, everyone stands to be dragged into this," he said. "Do you think for a moment she won't tell the papers how Dad paid her to pretend to be with me to smooth over what happened in Venice months ago?" He scoffed. "We're all in very real trouble."

Silence prevailed in the room, and then someone knocked. It didn't sound like Katya, and Eric moved to the door to open it. He was just as fluid as Louisa and Damien. Just as polished, with sandy hair that never sat out of place, and a pair of hazel eyes that observed everything.

Noah hadn't even asked Eric to help him get Zara's number. But Louisa had likely told her fiancé about Noah's feelings for Zara and how she couldn't help him. But that didn't mean Eric couldn't provide some assistance....

"They're ready for you," a woman said. "Should I tell them you'll be another minute?"

"No," Louisa said. "We're ready too." She turned back to Noah. "Don't forget your phone, baby brother."

She gave him a smile as she crossed the room toward him. She fiddled and fixed with his tie, though it was absolutely perfect. "I'm so sorry," she whispered. "But let's get through this event and then figure out what to do. Okay?"

Noah nodded. "Okay." Then he picked up his phone and followed his sister out of the room.

Two hours later, he rode in the back of the limousine, his sole focus on his phone as he tapped out a message to Zara. He had so much he wanted to say, but he decided to start small.

Hey, it's Noah. I have a new phone, and I'm sort of under a lot of stress. Can't talk much, but I've been thinking about you and hope your

He didn't know what to put there. He didn't want anyone to know he was texting Zara if they happened to look at his phone. So he didn't want to use her name. Or ask about her show. Or put anything personal that would help anyone connect any dots.

Which made his first communication with her in weeks utterly ridiculous.

He read over the message again, finishing it with, *I've been thinking about you and hope to see you really soon.*

Could he put a heart emoticon?

In the end, he didn't, just sending the words across the wide expanse of ocean and continents that separated them.

It was early morning in Getaway Bay, and a weekday, so Zara probably wouldn't have to be up too terribly early. He settled back into his seat, ready to wait a couple of hours to hear from her. Which made the vibration from his phone, indicating that he had a message, all the more thrilling as it moved through his fingers.

His heart beat in the back of his throat as he read her response.

Don't worry about it. Looks like you're having fun with Katya.

His blood ran cold. So she'd seen the Internet stories. What could he say to assure her this was fake without getting himself in trouble with his parents? Without throwing Eric under the bus?

I'm not, he sent.

A picture of him and Katya kissing was her response, along with the dreaded words, *Don't text me again, Noah. I've already moved on.*

Chapter Nineteen

Zara deleted Noah's texts, refusing to save his new number in her phone. He'd been gone for two weeks now, and every minute felt like someone trying to hollow her out the way they would a pumpkin.

You're fine, she told herself as she ran the dry floor mop along the entryway in the mansion. And she was fine. She had a good job. A lead part in a very successful show. Another opportunity as a dancer coming up in a luau this winter. And her friends and family.

She didn't need Prince Noah Wales.

In fact, ever since she'd met him, her life had been turned upside down and twisted inside out. She'd abandoned her friends, and her concentration at work had slipped.

She was better off without him.

Then why didn't she *feel* better? She wasn't sure, but

she knew she could figure it out and then make her text come true. She could figure out how to move on.

She finished the cleaning, packed her bag, and drove down to the amphitheater. She didn't need to be there for another hour, but Ian had asked her to come go over the plans for this new kind of production he wanted to put together. Part luau and part dance party, he actually wanted Zara to participate in the show but also help him direct it.

It was a great opportunity for her to expand her résumé, and she couldn't wait to get started. As she parked, her phone rang, and she really hoped it wasn't Katya again—or Noah. Perhaps he'd been with people earlier, and that was why he'd chosen to text instead of call after so much time had gone by. After all those pictures had been posted.

Did he think she wouldn't see them? That she wouldn't be worried that he'd basically fallen off the face of the planet?

Zara had learned that he didn't know Katya was texting her, and the other woman had never said how she'd gotten Noah's phone with all his contacts. But she was ruthless and relentless, and she made sure Zara saw every little thing going on in Noah's life, emphasizing how Zara wasn't a part of it and Katya was.

It wasn't Katya or Noah, but Shannon, Hope Sorensen's assistant. Zara answered with a very confused, "Hello?"

"Zara," Shannon said brightly. "It's Shannon from Your Tidal Forever?"

Even though her name had come up on the screen, Zara said, "Oh, hi, Shannon."

"I know this is a long shot, but I was wondering if you'd seen Holden Montego around the island? Someone said you'd dropped him off once or twice while he was volunteering for us."

Someone had seen them. Zara's mouth turned dry, and she wasn't even sure why. "I haven't seen him for a couple of weeks," she said truthfully.

"Oh, that's too bad," Shannon said, her voice definitely deflating. "We've got so much work to do, and I can't seem to get more volunteers in. He was such a good worker. Do you know if he's looking for a job? Hope's hiring a whole new construction crew."

Zara knew Holden was not looking for a job. And a lot more about him. But she just said, "I'm sorry, Shannon. I don't know. I don't think he's even in Getaway Bay anymore."

"Really?"

"I don't know," Zara said, because that seemed the safest answer.

"Okay, well, thanks. Sorry to bother you."

"No problem." Zara hung up and stared out the windshield. The conversation itself wasn't a problem, but the feelings and memories of Noah it stirred up certainly were. She hated that she didn't know if he'd be coming back, and then she reminded herself that she'd broken up with him only a few hours ago.

She didn't *want* him to come back, and his complete lack of response to her break-up text proved he didn't really care that much about her.

With her heart stinging in her chest, Zara got out of her car, shouldered her bag, and headed inside to meet with Ian. She didn't need Noah Wales. Oh, no, she did not. Maybe if she told herself that enough times, she'd start to believe it. Maybe it would even come true.

———

"SO HE'S JUST GONE?" SUZIE ASKED LATER THAT WEEK, the cup of coffee she'd insisted on getting before they could drive up to the mansion sitting abandoned on the table beside her.

"I think so," Zara said. She'd shut down every question and conversation about Noah over the past couple of weeks, but Suzie could be relentless in her pursuit of drama and details. She had a flair for gossip and she loved being involved in everything her friends did.

"How are you feeling?"

"Not great," Zara admitted.

"And he was really a prince?"

Zara had told Suzie all about her and Noah's little summer fling over the past couple of nights. Jill had started seeing Beni, and they went out with another group from the cast after the show, leaving Suzie to be Zara's sounding board since the break-up.

Zara knew she didn't mind, and she lifted her hot chocolate to her lips though it was still plenty warm in Getaway Bay. In fact, mid-July could be downright brutal. But they didn't sit by the pool tonight, choosing instead to lounge inside with the air conditioning and the comfy couches in the living room.

"He was really a prince," she said. "I knew him for a month. I don't know why I'm so hung up on him." She'd dated other guys for much longer.

"There's been no closure," Suzie said simply.

Zara almost rolled her eyes. "You've been talking to your brother about me."

"No," she said, her blue eyes sparkling with mischief. "Though if I did talk to Jeremiah, he'd say the same thing."

"He's a child psychologist."

"And he understands closure," Suzie shot back, the banter between them friendly and so welcome to Zara. She hated coming back to this big house alone, and Suzie had been staying over with her for a few nights now.

A few minutes went by, and then Zara finally said, "Closure," like she'd decided she did need some of that when it came to Noah. He hadn't texted again, but neither had Katya, and while one of those was a relief, Zara couldn't believe Noah had given up so easily.

Two texts, and he was done?

She'd thought he had more determination than that.

"You know, Miah hasn't dated anyone in a while," Suzie said.

Zara stood up with a groan. "I'm not going out with your brother."

"Why not?" Suzie picked up her unfinished coffee and followed Zara into the kitchen.

"Because I don't need to be set up," Zara said. "And he's not a nice Indian man." She smiled at Suzie. "Maybe I should just try to find someone my parents would approve of. I'm sure there's some very nice Indian men I could go out with."

Suzie stared at her, obviously dumbfounded. "Who are you? Where's Zee?"

Zara laughed and shook her head. "Come on. It's late, and we have another show tomorrow night." She stared down the hall, Suzie right beside her.

"Seriousy, Zee, I'm worried about you."

"I'm okay, Suze. Really, I am." She paused outside the bedroom her friend had been staying in. "I do miss him, but it's not like...." Her voice trailed off, unable to say what she wanted to say. *It's not like I was in love with him.*

But they had talked about him moving to the island permanently, and she'd taken him to meet her parents. That in itself was a very big deal, and Zara couldn't just dismiss it. She'd been willing to go through that terrible dinner, and so had Noah.

"Maybe just call him," Suzie said in a small voice. "See what he says."

Zara nodded just so she could escape to her own room. She didn't really think she'd call Noah. After all, she'd erased his texts from that new number, and he hadn't tried to get in touch with her again.

She wasn't the most technical person in the world, but she'd once helped her mother find out who Sai was texting by logging into their cell phone providers account and looking at the individual texts.

So she knew how to get the number. Instead of pulling out her laptop and doing that, she climbed into bed and stared at the ceiling, wondering where Noah was now and what he was doing.

It would be noon in Triguard, and he'd probably be lunching with a crowd of adoring fans. Then kissing Katya and laughing about everything that had happened in Getaway Bay with the clueless Indian girl who thought synchronized swimming was a career.

Zara rolled over, bitterness and heartbreak yanking through her hard enough to make tears come. And this time, she didn't push them back or hold them in. She cried, because she missed the man she had fallen in love with.

Chapter Twenty

N oah endured the last week of Louisa's engagement tour alone. It was better than trying to keep Katya's lips off of his, and certainly an improvement from the horrible situation he'd been put in.

But Zara's message had sent him into a tailspin he didn't know how to recover from. He clung to the tiny shred of hope that he'd be the perfect prince his father wanted, and then he'd get permission to leave this wretched island and make a new one his home.

Zara had said not to text her again, and Noah was planning to honor that. But he could call her or show up on her doorstep to talk to her. He just needed to get a few things in order first, and then he would.

The door he'd been sitting outside of opened, and his sister came out. She looked tired, but upbeat, and she gave him a hug after he stood up. "Your turn."

"How is he?" Noah asked, glancing toward his father's private office.

"He's...the king," Louisa said, which did not infuse any hope into Noah's heart. She walked away, her low heels and long skirt absolutely fitting for the princess she was. Noah tugged on his jacket sleeves and entered the office, determined to stay until he'd gotten what he wanted. No, what he needed.

"Father," he said once he'd entered, bowed, and closed the door.

"Noah, come and sit." His father smiled and removed his glasses. He seemed older than Noah remembered, and he took a few moments to really look at his dad. He couldn't even imagine what it would be like to shoulder the affairs of a country, even a small one like Triguard.

"How was the tour?"

Noah cocked his head. "Honestly, Father?"

"Honestly, Noah."

"It was terrible," Noah said. "Katya was a train wreck, and Zara broke up with me."

His father blinked as if Noah had just said it was going to rain later. "I'm sorry to hear that."

"Are you?" Noah hadn't meant to be disrespectful or negative. He drew in a deep breath. "It doesn't matter. I'll make things right with her." Just like he always made things right.

"Katya was a mistake."

"Thank you for saying so," Noah said. He wanted to

adjust his tie, but he held very still. Fidgeting showed nerves, and he didn't want his father to think he was anything less than poised and content.

"She won't be causing us any more problems." His father steepled his fingers and watched Noah.

"I'm happy to hear that."

"And now I suppose you want to know how you did on the tour, to see if I'm going to give you permission to live in Getaway Bay permanently."

Noah said nothing. The King had surely received daily reports from one of the people who'd traveled with the royal entourage on the engagement tour. He read six papers each day and spent an hour on the Internet too. He knew everything that happened in his kingdom, almost the moment it happened.

"I'm sorry to say I can't let you do that," he said, leaning back in his chair.

"Dad," Noah started, a whine plentiful in his voice. He cut off the sound and cleared his throat. "Why not?"

"Not for a few more months, at least," he said. "You just returned, and we need time to let the press move on to something else, the way they always do."

"A few more months?" A weight pressed on Noah's chest, making it difficult for his lungs to expand properly. "What's the difference if I hide out here in the castle or on the beach in Getaway Bay?"

He wanted to surf. He wanted to hold Zara and watch her complete that high dive. He wanted to be free from his royal obligations—and that was what his father couldn't grant.

"That's exactly the problem," his father said, confirming Noah's sudden realization. "You're not a normal man, Noah. You're a prince, and you have certain duties that come with that."

"Then I'll volunteer in libraries in Getaway Bay. They have a great children's hospital wing there. I'll donate money there and spend time there. I've already been volunteering on a celebrity wedding through one of their wedding planning businesses."

"Yes, Your Tidal Forever. I'm aware."

Of course he was. Noah didn't have anything else to say in his defense.

"I need you here for a while," he said. "Damien is launching a new health initiative, and he wants you to be the right-hand man."

"You mean he wants me to attend meetings and make speeches," Noah said. "Stay out of trouble."

"That's exactly what I mean. It will improve your image, and then you'll probably be able to return to Getaway Bay, as you wish to do. But we feel it's simply too soon for you to go now."

"I don't care about my image, Father."

"I realize that," he said dryly. "But we do, and as your reputation reflects on all of us, we've all suffered while you've been learning to surf in the Pacific Ocean."

A splash of shame moved through Noah. "No one

cares if I'm learning to surf or if I'm helping a child read."

"You're wrong about that," his dad said. "The child cares, and the child's mother cares, and the library director cares. And they're all citizens of this country. Citizens you're supposed to love and serve."

Noah could see he wasn't going to persuade his father into seeing things his way. He'd never been successful doing that in the past either. "Perhaps I could have a week," he said. "To travel to Getaway Bay, talk to Zara, and come back."

His dad laughed and shook his head. "I don't think so, Noah. I know you, and you're slipperier than an oiled eel. I let you out of my sight, and you'll be off the grid for who knows how long."

Noah stood, the meeting clearly over. "Well, Father, you knew I'd been learning to surf. You knew enough to send Damien on a 4-day round trip to find me. You knew where I was volunteering. Someone as smart and resourceful like you should be able to track me down pretty easily, should I not return." He buttoned his jacket and strode away from the desk though his father called him back.

He was not going to stay in Triguard for another few weeks. Because then it would be something else. Another month for this project. Then another six for holiday preparation. Then Louisa's wedding would be within a year, and there was no way he could leave then.

So he'd leave tonight. True, his father could cut off

all of his debit and credit cards, but Noah had allies inside the castle. He just needed to find them and convince them to help him.

Plus, he really needed to see Zara. Talk to her. Make her understand. And he wasn't going to wait another few months to do it.

———

"ARE YOU SURE?" NOAH ASKED LOUISA AS SHE SAT behind the wheel of a car. He'd never seen his sister drive, and he wasn't entirely sure she knew how.

"Yes, now be quiet." She looked at the dashboard in front of her like all she'd have to do was push a button and the vehicle would start. Noah was once again on the floor in the backseat, feeling too tall and too broad for such things.

His sister got the car started, and she eased it forward a little without jerking. So maybe she did know how to drive. They made it out of the huge shed where all the cars were kept and around the back of the castle before she stopped again.

Noah's pulse felt like it was part of a tennis match, bobbing to the left and then the right with great speed. "What's——"

The passenger door opened, and his brother said, "Are we all set?"

Before Noah could move, Damien looked over the seat. "You didn't even cover him up."

"We drove from the vehicle shed to here," Louisa snapped. "You said *you'd* bring something to cover him up."

Noah's heart warmed listening to his siblings bicker. In the end, Damien ended up running back up to the doors of his wing of the castle, and what felt like an hour later, he returned with one blanket. "It's all I could sneak away from Matzen," he said. "That man is like a bloodhound."

He draped the blanket over Noah, who experienced a strong sense of déjà vu. The drive to the gate happened quickly, and Louisa said, "We're just taking a drive to the seashore," as if she needed the guard's permission to do so. Once free of the Wales Family land, Noah kicked off the blanket and sat up in the backseat. He wanted to tell his brother and sister how much he appreciated them, and that he didn't want to leave Triguard because of them. He said nothing, as the family didn't have a custom of saying what they really felt.

At the airport, she avoided the section where the press were allowed to congregate, and instead, drove around the back of the airport to a place Noah had never been before.

"I've arranged a private flight for you," Damien said. "Straight through to Getaway Bay, with a stop in Toronto for refueling. You won't even get off the plane, though." He turned and looked at Noah, his features serious.

"Thank you, Damien."

"I hope it works out with Zara," he said. "She seems very important to you."

Noah nodded and said, "She is. I hope I'll be able to fix the situation with her." He thought of her stubborn streak and how traditional her family was. But he was willing to do almost anything to be with her, including defying his father and sneaking away in broad daylight.

His sister got out of the car and grabbed onto him. "Be safe, Noah," she said.

"You're the ones who are going to get filleted alive," he whispered. "All three heirs in a car with no security?"

She looked like a scared rabbit as she ducked back into the car and drove off, a final wave from Damien the last thing Noah saw before he faced the jet sitting before him. Three people waited at the bottom of the stairs, and Noah approached them.

"Prince Noah," the older man said. "I'll be your pilot for the first leg of our journey. My name is Roberto. Antonio will take us from Toronto to Hawaii after we've refueled. And Mary will help you in the cabin with whatever you need." He nodded Noah onto the plane, which was much better than the regular commercial flight he'd taken to get to Triguard.

He was the only passenger besides the three his brother had hired to get him back to Getaway Bay, and he suddenly didn't feel so bad for Damien and his trip to Getaway Bay weeks ago. This plane had a huge bed, as well as two recliners flanking it, and Noah chose one of those for the first part of the flight.

He slept as well as he would've in the mansion, and by the time they landed in Getaway Bay, Noah knew he would never fly on any other plane but this one. He gave all three people a large tip and stepped into the glorious Hawaiian sunshine.

Yes, it was still hot in Getaway Bay. Yes, there were still too many tourists. But as he accepted a flower lei and got in line to wait for a taxi, there was nowhere he'd rather be.

His phone took a few minutes to update to local time, and as he waited, he wondered where he could find Zara at two o'clock in the afternoon. Did she go to work that early, if the show didn't start until seven?

Noah had no plan for how to approach her, or what to say. So when he got in the back of a cab, with only his backpack and wallet, and the driver asked him where to go, Noah said, "Indian House."

He wasn't sure what he'd find at her family's restaurant, but there was no one who knew Zara better than her family.

The moment he stepped inside, a woman gasped and said, "Prince Noah," and he thought he'd been discovered. But it was only Zara's sister, Abi, and she had both hands covering her mouth.

"Hey," he said. "I just need a table in the corner and access to the Internet. Do you think you could help me?"

"What are you doing here?" She plucked a menu from the podium but didn't move.

"I need to figure out how to get Zara back."

Abi grinned like he'd just passed the biggest test of his life and said, "Right this way." She indeed led him to the very corner of the restaurant and he sat with his back to everything.

She put the menu in front of him, and he said, "Bring me the butter chicken, would you?"

"Of course. And the WiFi password is swimmergirl."

Noah looked up, surprised. Abi shrugged and said, "My parents are very proud people," as if that explained everything. Maybe it did.

He nodded and pulled out his laptop, determined to do whatever he could to get tickets to her show. If not that night, then as soon as possible. And he was going to show up and surprise her, apologize until she forgave him, and kiss her until he couldn't breathe.

Oh, and then he needed to go get his dog from the guy who'd agreed to take him while Noah had been out of town. He'd met Tyler on the beach, and he had two dogs with him that Boomer had really liked. He hadn't been able to text Tyler either, but he seemed like the laid-back type of surfer dude who wouldn't mind keeping a good dog for a few weeks.

He flexed his fingers. "I just need tickets," he muttered to himself. By the time the butter chicken came and he'd consumed it, he still hadn't found even a single ticket for the foreseeable future.

So maybe he needed a miracle instead.

Chapter Twenty-One

Zara bounced on the balls of her feet, ready to get this show started. But there had been a lighting glitch, and they'd been delayed for fifteen minutes. She'd sat in the whirlpool to stay warm, and now she just wanted to *go*.

Though she was behind the closed door in the locker room, when Suzie came bursting through it, Zara heard the noise outside. "What's going on?" she asked, trying to get a peek before the door closed. "How close are they?"

Suzie pressed her back into the door, a grin filling her whole face. "They're close. There's just...Maine Fitzgerald showed up, and everyone's making a big deal out of it."

Zara's heart stuttered a little, though she had no chance with quarterback Maine Fitzgerald. He was dating someone, and had been for a long time. But still. A celebrity at Fresh Start.

She'd performed in the show dozens of times now, and still she felt jittery. A few minutes later someone knocked on the door and said, "Two minutes, Zee."

After snapping her goggles into place, she eased into the pool that would get her out to the arena without being seen. She held onto the platform, she rode it up high, and she and Beni performed their spectacular dives into the pool below.

She usually came up to thunderous applause, but tonight, when she broke the surface of the water, only silence rained down on her. Sliding up onto the edge of the pool as normal, she waved as though they were cheering like they'd just seen her win the Super Bowl.

A man stood up and a spotlight shone on him. Zara's hand froze mid-wave and she felt like she'd just inhaled a lungful of salt water.

It was Noah Wales. Prince Noah Wales.

Right there, just on the other side of the railing. Maybe ten feet from her. He lifted his hand in a wave and called, "Amazing, Zara!" He started to applaud, and his third clap got swallowed by the crowd as they all joined him on their feet, the roof-shaking applause now what she was accustomed to.

She didn't know what to do. The timing of the show was off now, and she still perched on the edge of the pool. Finally, someone grabbed onto her ankles and said, "Come on, Zee. You can talk to him after."

Zara joined Suzie in the water, and she missed the first synchronized move with the other girls but managed to get her leg up on the second one. Her heart skipped every third beat, and she couldn't hold her breath as long as she used to.

Noah was here.

What was Noah *doing* here?

She wanted to go see him during intermission, but she found the exits blocked by James, Beni, and Ian himself.

"After the show," Ian said. "I already did him a *huge* favor by moving his seat, and postponing the show so he could get situated right where you'd come out of the water."

"*You* did that?" Zara stared at him in disbelief. And now she'd have to put her swim cap back on over wet hair and skin, and that was a huge pain.

"Well, the lights were already a problem, so I figured what was a few more minutes?" Ian shrugged and smiled, and added, "He seems like a really great guy, for what it's worth."

Zara wasn't sure what she thought. She didn't really want to see Noah, but he was here. On the island. And she wanted to find out how he'd achieved that. And fine, she wanted to find out if they could have a second chance.

But first she had to finish the second act of her show. As she did, she couldn't help thinking that the name of this production was Fresh Start—and that was exactly what she and Noah needed.

After the final applause, after she'd showered and

changed, after she had everything in her bag ready to go, Zara sat on the thin benches in the locker room and stared at her phone. Almost everyone else had left, and her nerves prevented her from doing the same.

"Come *on*," Suzie hissed from the doorway leading into the hall. "What are you doing?"

Zara lifted one shoulder in a shrug and looked at her best friend. "I don't know."

"Don't you at least want to hear how he got here?"

"I don't know," Zara said. She did, but she didn't at the same time. "What if he has to leave again in the morning?" She'd already started piecing her heart back together. It hadn't gone well, and she still had a lot of cracks and wounds to heal, but she'd started.

Suzie entered the locker room, looking like she could eat kittens for breakfast. "Zara, come on. He's all you've talked about for a week, and I know you were suffering in silence before that. So he's here. And he's *gorgeous*. And he's just as nervous as you. So come *on*." She tugged on Zara's hand hard enough to get her to stand.

Zara moved to the door, only because Suzie was behind her and she couldn't turn and flee the other way.

She'd taken one step into the hall when Suzie added, "And besides, your family needs to get back to the restaurant."

"My family?" The last word whispered out of Zara's mouth, because she'd seen Noah. And he was wonderful and strong and everything she held in her memory of him.

He took an anxious step forward, a huge bouquet of flowers in his hands. Sure enough, her family—her parents, both sets of grandparents, all her sisters and their husbands, and her aunties and uncles—flanked him.

Zara could hardly move, but her wooden legs managed to get her down the hall to a more open area where everyone stood.

"Hey, Zara," Noah said, his warm, deep voice washing over her. Soothing her. So not fair. She wanted to be mad at him, and he'd charmed her simply by saying her name. "These are for you. Your sister said you like carnations the best."

"She does," Krisha said.

"But they smell bad," Abi said. "He should've gotten hibiscus."

"There's some of those too," he said. "Your friend Ash helped me get them. I guess her fiancé owns a flower business?"

Zara nodded and took the bouquet. She did love carnations, and she did like the way hibiscus smelled. "How long have you been back?"

"I got here about noon," he said.

Her eyebrows went up. "And you mobilized my family and met my friend Ash?"

"I was a little late to the show," he said, a magnificent smile touching his mouth. Zara wanted to touch his mouth. Feel him and make sure he was real and not a mirage. "It took *forever* to get a ticket."

"How *did* you get a ticket?" she asked.

"I called Ian."

Of course he did. Only Prince Noah would be able to figure to call in a favor to a man he barely knew. Bold. The fact that he'd been able to orchestrate everything so perfectly felt like she'd entered an alternate reality.

"After my lunch of butter chicken," he said. "Things got really interesting. I wasn't going to do all of this. I just wanted to see you." He took a step forward, his hand reaching toward her like he wanted to make sure she was real too.

"I wanted to apologize," he said. "I'm sure you've seen some things online that have been upsetting. I know I need to explain and earn your trust back." He glanced at her father, who nodded once.

"But I'm in love with you Zara Reddy, and I'll do whatever it takes to make things right between us." He dropped to one knee and took the black jewelry box from her mother in one quick movement.

Zara couldn't breathe. It seemed to take an hour for Noah to crack that lid. When he did, he presented the glittering, diamond ring to her and asked, "Will you marry me?"

Sai and Myra sighed like they were Disney princesses, but tears stung Zara's eyes. She wanted to look to her parents for permission, but their presence meant they'd already given it.

So she nodded, some of her tears splashing down her face, and said, "Yes, Noah. I'll marry you."

He grinned and fumbled a little to remove the ring from the box and slide it on her finger. Then he stood, took the flowers and handed them to someone, and gathered her into the safety of his strong arms.

"I'm so sorry," he murmured just before lowering his head and kissing her. Zara knew there was a lot to talk about still, but it didn't seem to matter all that much. He was here, and he'd fixed a lot already.

So she kissed him back, hoping her actions could convey the three little words she'd yet to say.

Her family and friends cheered, and it was the exact proposal Zara had never known she wanted. She pulled away, giggling, and Noah tucked her into his side while they faced her parents.

Her mother wore a smile and wiped at her eyes, and that set Zara to crying all over again. She hugged her mom, who asked, "You will do the traditional Indian wedding, yes?"

"Nita, give her a few days," her dad said, drawing Zara into his embrace. "Congratulations, Zee. You two will be so happy."

She wondered what had changed their minds, but she decided she had plenty of time to find out. She hugged her sisters, her aunties, and everyone else before returning to find Noah had picked up her swim bag and was holding her flowers.

"Do you want to see where I live?" he asked.

"Don't tell me you found a house since noon too."

She looked at him, pure shock moving through her. Was there anything he couldn't do?

He shrugged and said, "You might want to use the bathroom before we go."

Chapter Twenty-Two

N oah laid on his back, the sand soft beneath him, and stared at the stars, thanking each one for his reunion with Zara.

She lay curled into his side, and neither of them spoke. The slight scent of chlorine mingled with flowers, and it was the best smell in the whole world.

"What did your father say?" she asked to break the silence between them.

"I haven't spoken to him since sneaking away." He'd told her the whole story of his time in Triguard, his horrible experience with Katya, and how he feared his father would never allow him to return to Getaway Bay.

"I'm sure he was livid with Louisa and Damien."

"I would like to meet them," she said.

"You will. We'll go visit my parents, and we'll of course go for her wedding, but that won't be for, like, ever."

"Really?"

"Oh, the royal engagements are ridiculous."

"I would like a short engagement," Zara said, and Noah smiled at the stars.

"That's fine with me, sweetheart."

"I'll talk to my mother tomorrow. See what we can put on the calendar."

"You might need to explain to me what a traditional Indian wedding looks like."

"Oh, we won't have a traditional Indian wedding."

Noah's arm around her tightened. "We won't?"

"I'll wear the traditional clothing, and it'll be loud. Every party we have is very loud. But it won't be full-blown traditional."

"But we can have butter chicken, right?"

Zara giggled, her breath heating his skin beneath his T-shirt. "I suppose we can have butter chicken."

The sky above them held magic, and Noah wanted to stay on this island for the rest of his life.

"Did you know Katya had your phone?" she asked, and Noah flinched.

"What do you mean?"

"I mean, she had your phone and she texted me. She was the one who sent me the picture of you two kissing."

Noah hated the sound of those words coming out of Zara's mouth, and he pressed his eyes closed. "My mother dropped my phone in the koi pond."

"Well, when I texted you to ask you a question, she responded."

"What did she say?"

"I don't know." She took a deep breath. "All kinds of stuff. She was basically bragging about how she was with you and I wasn't."

"You know she was never 'with me,' right?"

"Yes," she said, and it was the best word he'd ever heard. She lifted her head and added, "Come on. You told me you'd show me your place."

"It's too dark," he said.

A beat of silence passed, and then she said, "You don't have electricity?"

"Well...."

"And no running water."

"Nope."

"You're moving back into the mansion."

"No, I'm not."

"Noah." She pushed up on her elbow. "Where do you go to the bathroom?"

"There's a bathroom down the beach a bit," he said. "There's showers and a sink and stuff."

"It's not private."

"I don't mind."

"There's got to be somewhere you can live that has the things you need."

Noah gently drew her back into his side. "I'm sure you're right. I'll find somewhere tomorrow."

"And where's Boomer?" she asked.

"I met a guy named Tyler?" Noah said, like it was a question. "He said he'd take him."

"Tyler Rigby? The billionaire poker player?"

"I have no idea."

"You gave Boomer to a stranger." Zara shook her head against his chest. "I can't believe you."

"He had two other dogs, and he seemed chill."

"Definitely Tyler Rigby."

"Do you have his number then?"

"I'm sure I can figure out how to get in touch with him. I think he's friends with Ash's husband."

"Because I lost all my contacts when I got a new phone, and I don't exactly know how to get in touch with him."

Zara started giggling, and Noah couldn't help but join in. He wanted this life with her, laughing at the moonlight and snuggling on the sand. He wanted electricity and indoor plumbing too, and he decided that tomorrow, finding a functional place to live was priority one.

The next morning, when he finally dragged himself out of bed, he found his phone laden with messages. He read the ones from Zara, Louisa, and Damien, and ignored the ones from his parents.

He asked Zara for Tyler's number, and a few minutes later he was able to text the man about getting Boomer back. While he had Tyler's attention, he asked about a real estate agent, and an hour later, he walked into an office that looked more like a beach hideaway to find a woman sitting behind a desk.

"I'm looking for Jewel," he said.

"Oh, I'm Jewel." She tossed her long, blonde hair as she stood. "You must be Noah." She extended her hand across the desk, and they shook hands.

"That I am," he said. "And I really need a new place as fast as possible." He thought about the hammock he'd slept in last night. No way he could let Zara see where he called home.

"Let's talk for a few minutes, and I'll see what I've got." She settled behind her desk again, and Noah took the chair across from her. "What are we looking at for budget?"

Noah hadn't checked his accounts, and had no idea if they were still operational, but he said, "The budget is wide open."

Jewel didn't blink. "Size?"

"Nothing huge," he said. "Something normal, for a normal person. I am getting married soon, though, so something for two normal people. And maybe a family." He realized he was rambling, and he pressed his lips together in a closed-mouth smile.

"On the beach? A condo? I've got a couple of things up on the bluff." Jewel glanced at him.

"Not the bluff," he said. "My parents have a place up there, and I'd prefer to be down on the beach anyway. Not a condo. I have a dog, and he likes to go outside like, every five seconds."

"Large yard for the dog?"

He could hire a gardener, or better yet, figure out

how to push a mower himself. "Sure," he said. "Or not. The yard doesn't matter to me."

"Pool?"

He thought of Zara, and started nodding. "Definitely."

Jewel tapped and clicked and smiled. "I think I have the perfect place for you." She beamed at him, printed one sheet of paper and said, "Do you want to follow me?"

He nodded, his heart bobbing around in the back of his throat. He'd never purchased a house of his own, and he couldn't wait to see what Jewel had for him. And there was just the one, so he hoped it was available right away.

She drove for about ten minutes before turning into a perfectly normal neighborhood, with completely ordinary homes. She parked in the driveway, which would accommodate four cars, and got out. "Here it is. The house is vacant, so you'll have to use your imagination for where furniture would be." She clicked toward the front porch. "But the whole thing has recently been painted, and there's new carpet throughout."

Noah didn't care about the carpet or the paint. The house screamed normal, and it had five bedrooms and four bathrooms, which was plenty of room for him, Boomer, and Zara, even if they had a family.

It was the pool and yard that sold him the moment he stepped onto the back patio. While the house was in a neighborhood, it sat on the edge of it and the backyard stretched for a good distance before the sand took over.

"Do we own the beach?"

"Unfortunately, no," Jewel said. "But there is access, and not many people come to the beach if they don't live in the neighborhood."

He glanced at the sparkling pool, which a tall, vinyl fence surrounded to provide some privacy. "I'll take it."

"Really?" Jewel asked. "Just like that?"

"Just like that." Noah smiled at her. "Is that not how people do it?" His grin slipped. "This is my first time buying a house."

"It is?"

"Yes." Did it really show?

"Well, you'll get some incentives for that." She pulled her phone from her purse. "Let me put in an offer." She babbled on about the price of the house and how it really was quite fair, but that the owners had left the island already and were desperate to sell. "So we could probably go in lower." She looked at Noah, obviously asking him.

He had no idea. "I'm fine with the list price," he said. "And I'd love to move in like, tonight."

Jewel's eyebrows went up. "Well, I'm afraid that won't happen, Mister Wales. We have to do the financing, and the inspection, and—"

"I'm willing to buy it as-is," he said. "With cash. Today."

Jewel gaped at him, the hand holding her phone falling to her side. "Cash?" wisped out of her mouth.

"Today," he said.

She regained her professionalism and said, "Let me call the real estate agent for the owners. Perhaps we can work out an agreement that allows you immediate occupancy in exchange for no inspection and a full cash offer."

Noah nodded at her, imagining himself living in this house…with Zara. In fact, he wanted to marry her right there in that gorgeous backyard, with the banyan trees above them and the beach beyond them. He even knew who to hire to make her wedding dreams come true.

He shook away the fantasies and focused on the moment. He first had to make sure he had the cash in liquid form to buy this place. Then he could bring Zara here and ask her what she thought of tying the knot with him right there in this new, normal place they could call their own.

Six Months Later

"**M**other," Zara said in a somewhat reproving voice. "Does the music need to be quite so loud?"

She stood in Noah's house—which would soon be her house too—and let her sisters make sure all the pieces of her traditional *lehnga*, which Ash had sewn beautifully, fit and laid right. They wove flowers through her hair, and Sai was currently painting her right arm in intricate henna swirls. Zara's left arm was already done, and the wedding was only an hour away now.

"It is a party," her mother said in response.

Zara rolled her eyes, but she didn't say anything else. She had to live in this neighborhood, and while Noah had been here for a while and said the neighbors were nice, not everyone enjoyed Indian music at ten o'clock in the morning.

There would be the ceremony, and then a huge

luncheon, which Indian House had catered. The restaurant was closed for the day, and Zara had appreciated her parents so much over the past few months as they'd planned the wedding.

No, Noah was not a nice Indian man, but he was a handsome prince. He was *her* handsome prince, and she couldn't wait to see him in his traditional tuxedo and the royal blue and purple tie every man in the Wales family wore to get married.

So they were blending their two worlds, and Zara got a little weepy just thinking about it. She'd flown to Triguard to meet his parents a few months ago, and they were lovely people. Stuffy, as Noah called them, but polite and kind and absolutely accommodating.

They'd arrived on the island about three weeks ago, and Zara had been up to the mansion for dinner with them several times as the wedding approached. His sister and her fiancé were staying in an undisclosed location around the point of the island, and his brother, the Crown Prince of Triguard was staying in a third location with a full security detail.

Noah loved his siblings, and when the three of them were together, Zara could feel the camaraderie between them. Louisa had treated Zara like a sister from the first moment they'd met, and she'd admitted she'd wanted to be the first one to get married, but that everything in Triguard seemed to take an eternity.

"So many details," she said. "And Mother keeps changing her mind."

Zara didn't understand that, as her mother had a set of rules and cultural traditions that Zara had to continually modify.

"Finished," Sai said, and Zara realized the two of them were alone. "You look so beautiful, Zara."

"Thanks, Sai," she said, smiling at the sister just older than her. "Did Mark come?"

Her sister's dark eyes shone from within. "He sure did. I hope he'll see that it's possible to be normal and be Indian too."

Zara laughed, as Noah had an obsession with being normal, and when she'd suggested they get married in Triguard, with the whole royal affair, he'd immediately said no. He wanted a normal wedding, and he'd somehow gotten it into his mind that the ceremony should take place in his backyard.

Which was fine with Zara, honestly. She just wanted to get married, and she didn't need all the fanfare. However, his parents had asked them to please come to Triguard after their honeymoon so the people there could congratulate the couple.

Noah had said it would be more than a party, but a whole parade with pomp and cheering and gifts galore.

Zara wouldn't be a princess, but his father had declared her with the title of Her Royal Highness, the Duchess of Oceania, and Noah was now His Royal Highness, the Duke of Oceania. She honestly had no idea what the titles meant, but she was happy his family had come to terms with her and Noah's relationship.

"Ready?" her mom asked, bustling back into the room. Shannon came with her, and she looked a little frazzled, which was saying something. The wedding planner rarely looked anything but calm and cool, but she probably didn't know what to do with all of Zara's family's crazy traditions. Or how those were in complete contrast to Noah's family and their demeanor during a wedding.

Zara looked down at her arms, still covered in henna. "No, Sai just finished and this isn't dry yet."

"It can come off," Sai said, collecting a washcloth. She worked quickly, and her mother fussed around Zara for another few minutes before declaring her the perfect Indian bride.

She met her father on the back patio and found the backyard full of chairs and tents. It was windy today, but no one seemed to notice, and the music quieted enough for people to realize she'd arrived and the ceremony was beginning.

She'd asked her dad to walk her down the aisle, which was more of a Western tradition, and they stepped slowly toward Noah, who stood at an altar he'd made himself. Zara kept her eyes on him and let the joy flow through her.

Her father kissed both of her cheeks before passing her to Noah, who looked dashing and dreamy in his tuxedo. His family sat together on the front row, every one of them proper and perfect.

Zara felt perfect too, and she listened as the pastor

promised them wealth and health if they turned to each other to work through the storms of life. When he got to the vows, Zara looked at Noah and squeezed both of his hands.

How she'd gotten lucky enough to catch his eye, she'd never know. But when it was her turn to say, "I do," she did so in a loud voice, glad when Noah repeated the words to her.

Then he tipped her back and kissed her, which caused the onlookers to erupt in cheers. The music blared again, and Zara held onto Noah's face a moment longer, whispering the words, "I love you, Noah, my perfect prince."

He grinned, kissed her again, and said, "I love you too."

—————

Read on for sneak peek at THE ISLAND RETREAT, Book 4 in the Getaway Bay series.

Sneak Peek! The Island Retreat
Chapter One

"All right, guys." Shannon Bell put her purse over her shoulder and clicked her way toward the front door. "Be good while I'm at work." She flashed a bright smile to her two cats, both of whom sat at perfect attention a few feet away.

Of course, neither of them responded to her, and Shannon went out the door and down the steps. She had a routine she followed each morning, and she was right on schedule to hit Roasted at their slowest time between eight and nine.

She'd tried different times, and eight-twenty in the morning seemed to be the best time to get her daily dose of caffeine before she had to go to work at Your Tidal Forever. She loved her job, though it was a bit intense from time to time.

"At least the celebrity wedding and the royal wedding

are over," she told herself as she buckled her seatbelt and started her car. She loved this car, and she lowered the top to let in the spring sunshine as she started toward downtown Getaway Bay.

She hooked her purse over her arm as she walked into the coffee shop, running her fingers through her hair to tame some of the messy curls back into waves. Only four people waited in line, and Shannon smiled to herself that she'd timed her coffee shop visit exactly right again.

Shannon prided herself on the details of things. It was what made her a good secretary, and why Hope Sorensen at Your Tidal Forever had told Shannon she could never quit.

Her body was still recovering from the high-profile weddings over the past couple of months, and she wished she wasn't such a night owl. That, or she needed another job where she didn't have to be to work by nine.

But she had a secretarial degree and a professional certification in organization. So she was well-suited for the many moving parts a wedding planning business required, and she'd enjoyed her last five years at Your Tidal Forever.

Well, most of the time she enjoyed the work. Sometimes Hope could be a little intense, and when they had two of the biggest celebrities tying the knot one month, and then a prince getting married only a couple later, there had been times that Shannon felt like she'd lose her mind with all the tiny pieces that needed to be finished on time.

In the five minutes she waited to put in her order for a large caramel mocha, the bell on the door rang eight more times, and she asked for a cranberry orange bran muffin too, as she rarely ate breakfast before she left the house.

With summer right around the corner, Shannon had dozens of tasks to complete that day, and she'd be lucky if she got fifteen minutes for lunch. Maybe she could get Riley to get food for everyone, or she'd just run down the boardwalk to the Ohana Resort, which had recently opened a shop that served soups, salads, and sandwiches for the professional lunch crowd. The Lunch Spot promised food in ten minutes or less, and they had dozens of tables in the sand that always seemed full.

She got her coffee and turned to leave. Her eyes scanned the line of people waiting, catching on a tall, good-looking man she'd seen every day for a long time. She couldn't pinpoint when she'd first met Doctor Jeremiah Yeates, or when she'd learned his name, or when she'd realized that he worked in the building just down from Your Tidal Forever.

It seemed like they'd known each other for a while, and she waved to him as she passed.

"You beat me today," he said with a smile, and she couldn't help the little laugh that came out of her mouth. She quelled it by sipping her coffee, because while she and Jeremiah were friendly, there had never been much of a spark there.

She knew his name and where he worked. That was

all. They could probably ride to work together if they wanted to, but neither of them had ever brought it up. And Shannon wasn't going to today either.

Yes, Jeremiah was handsome and clearly well-off, as Shannon never saw him wearing anything but an expensive suit, and when he got to Roasted before her, she'd noticed that he bought coffee for his whole office.

Every morning, the man bought coffee for his whole office. Shannon couldn't even imagine Hope doing that, though the owner did sometimes bring in food, but usually for clients and the employees just ate what was left over.

As Hope walked across the parking lot to her car, her purse swinging and the coffee in her hand a bit too warm to really drink. Shannon was more of a lukewarm coffee lover, and she probably wouldn't touch her brew for another hour at least.

She found a couple standing at the front corner of her car, and she glanced at him, a blip of anxiety flipping through her. She clicked her keys to unlock the car, though the top on the convertible was still down and if there had been anything worth stealing inside, it probably would've been gone by now.

The couple moved away, and Shannon glanced at the front of her beloved car. It was fine. Of course it was fine. Getaway Bay didn't have a high crime rate, and Shannon didn't really have anything to be worried about.

Except the flat tire staring back at her.

"Oh, no," she said, the words part of a much larger

moan. She opened the door and put her purse inside, as well as her coffee. Then she placed her hands on her hips and faced the tire. Her father had taught her how to change a flat tire, as well as her oil, but Shannon never used the lessons. She had money, and why should she shimmy under her car when Max could do it at the lube shop for thirty bucks?

But Max wasn't here now, and Shannon had a ton to do at work. She opened her trunk and pulled back the roof to reveal the spare tire. She had no idea if she had the right tools to change a tire, but she was going to find out.

She found a X-shaped tool that she seemed to recall her father using to loosen the bolts. Bolts? That didn't seem like the right term, but Shannon literally made appointments, took messages, and tasted wedding cakes for a living.

The tool fit over the bolts, and she twisted. Nothing happened. After several more minutes of straining and trying to get even one of those stupid bolts off, and sweat poured down Shannon's face. Her blouse had come untucked and she had no idea where her heels were.

She crouched next to the tire, frustration about to make her say or do something she'd likely regret later— like calling her father for help.

"Can't do it," she said, and she also regretted her skirt choice, as this one was a little snug along her waist and hips.

"Need some help?" a man asked, and Shannon startled toward the deep, familiar voice. She twisted and peered up at none other than Jeremiah Yeates and the two trays of coffee he held in his hands.

"I have a flat tire," she said, trying to straighten.

Horror struck her like lightning at the sound of a seam *riiipping*, and she spun to put her backside against her cherry red convertible.

To Jeremiah's great credit, he acted like she hadn't just split her skirt open and stepped over to the hood of the car, where he set down the seven cups of coffee. "I think I can change a tire."

"I haven't been able to get off the bolts," she said, wiping her bangs off her forehead. Her hand came away wet, and more embarrassment squirreled through her.

"Let's see what I can do with these lug nuts," Jeremiah said, taking his suit coat off and draping it over the driver's side door. He wore a light blue, short-sleeved dress shirt, and Shannon couldn't help but admire the width of his shoulders and the obvious strength in his biceps.

Shannon looked away, her heart pounding a bit harder than normal for a reason she couldn't identify. So Jeremiah spent some time in the gym. So did a lot of men.

He picked up the tool she'd been wrestling with and crouched where she'd been. With the first yank on the wrench, the bolt—lug nut, whatever—came loose, and Shannon felt another blast of humiliation.

Jeremiah made short work of the lug nuts and pulled the full-size tire off. "Yeah, it looks like you drove over a nail," he said.

"Oh," she said. "I live over in the Cliff Cove area, and they're doing some construction up there."

"Yeah," he said with a big grin. "I live up there too."

Surprise pulled through her. "You do?"

"Yeah, off White Sails Lane."

That was only a few blocks from her, and she said, "I'm off Five Island."

His smile was glorious and beautiful, and why hadn't Shannon ever noticed it before? She tucked her dark hair behind her ear, wishing the sun didn't make her whole head feel like it was ablaze.

"I'm going to be so late for work," she said. "I'm so sorry. Are you—do you have a patient this morning?"

"I'm okay," he said, walking to the back of the car to get the spare tire. "Let me text my secretary real quick." He pulled his phone out and started sending a message, prompting Shannon to do the same thing. Hope couldn't blame her for being late if she had a flat tire. In fact, Shannon beat Hope to the office every day anyway.

"Shannon?" he asked from the trunk, and Shannon looked up from her phone.

"Yeah?"

"I don't think this spare is any good." He glanced at her and back into the trunk.

She shimmied along the side of the car and placed

her palm flat against her backside as she turned to stand right beside him. She peered into the trunk too, asking, "What's wrong with it?"

"Look how it's cracked along the side there?" He ran his finger along the edge of the tire. "We can't put this on."

She appreciated the use of "we," but she had absolutely no idea what to do now.

"I can give you a ride to work," he said. "And maybe you can call someone to come tow the car and get the tire fixed?" He looked at her like she had resources to do that. And she did, but she didn't want to call her dad and admit she couldn't change her own tire.

"All right," she said. "Are you sure it's okay?"

Jeremiah grinned at her. "It's no problem, Shannon," he said. "We work right next door to each other, and I just found out you're like, three blocks away from where I live." He hefted the flat tire into her trunk and slammed it closed. "So it's absolutely no problem."

Shannon couldn't help returning his smile, because it was just so dashing, and he was so good-looking, and he smelled like cologne and sunshine and dark roast coffee.

As she collected her purse and coffee and walked with him over to his car, Shannon wondered why she'd never looked at Doctor Jeremiah Yeates more than once on her way out of the coffee shop.

———

Oh, a doctor, a flat tire, and a coffee shop? Yes, please! Find out what happens with Jeremiah and Shannon in **THE ISLAND RETREAT, which is available in paperback, ebook, or audiobook.**

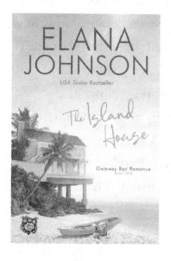

The Island House (Book 1): Charlotte Madsen's whole world came crashing down six months ago with the words, "I met someone else."

Can Charlotte navigate the healing process to find love again?

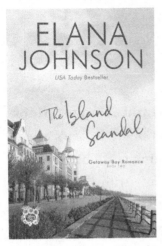

The Island Scandal (Book 2): Ashley Fox has known three things since age twelve: she was an excellent seamstress, what her wedding would look like, and that she'd never leave the island of Getaway Bay. Now, at age 35, she's been right about two of them, at least.

Can Burke and Ash find a way to navigate a romance when they've only ever been friends?

The Island Hideaway (Book 3): She's 37, single (except for the cat), and a synchronized swimmer looking to make some extra cash. Pathetic, right? She thinks so, and she's going to spend this summer housesitting a cliffside hideaway and coming up with a plan to turn her life around.

Can Noah and Zara fight their feelings for each other as easily as they trade jabs? Or will this summer shape up to be the one that provides the romance they've each always wanted?

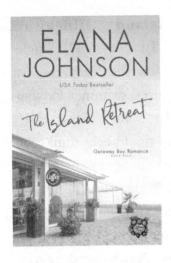

The Island Retreat (Book 4): Shannon's 35, divorced, and the highlight of her day is getting to the coffee shop before the morning rush. She tells herself that's fine, because she's got two cats and a past filled with emotional abuse. But she might be ready to heal so she can retreat into the arms of a man she's known for years...

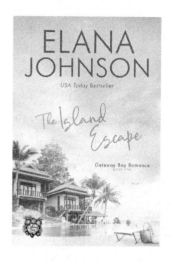

The Island Escape (Book 5): Riley Randall has spent eight years smiling at new brides, being excited for her friends as they find Mr. Right, and dating by a strict set of rules that she never breaks. But she might have to consider bending those rules ever so slightly if she wants an escape from the island...

The Island Storm (Book 6): Lisa is 36, tired of the dating scene in Getaway Bay, and practically the only wedding planner at her company that hasn't found her own happy-ever-after. She's tried dating apps and blind dates...but could the company party put a man she's known for years into the spotlight?

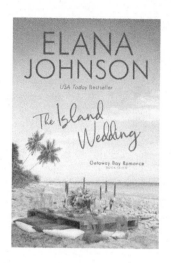

The Island Wedding (Book 7): Deirdre is almost 40, estranged from her teenaged daughter, and determined not to feel sorry for herself. She does the best she can with the cards life has dealt her and she's dreaming of another island wedding...but it certainly can't happen with the widowed Chief of Police.

Books in the Getaway Bay Resort Romance series

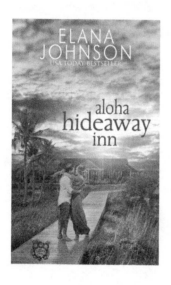

Aloha Hideaway Inn (Book 1): Can Stacey and the Aloha Hideaway Inn survive strange summer weather, the arrival of the new resort, *and* the start of a special relationship?

Getaway Bay (Book 2): Can Esther deal with dozens of business tasks, unhappy tourists, *and* the twists and turns in her new relationship?

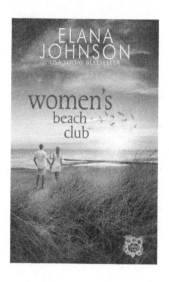

Women's Beach Club (Book 3): With the help of her friends in the Beach Club, can Tawny solve the mystery, stay safe, and keep her man?

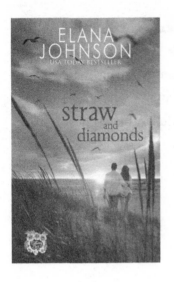

Straw and Diamonds (Book 4): Can Sasha maintain her sanity amidst their busy schedules, her issues with men like Jasper, and her desires to take her business to the next level?

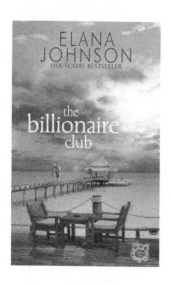

The Billionaire Club (Book 5): Can Lexie keep her business affairs in the shadows while she brings her relationship out of them? Or will she have to confess everything to her new friends...and Jason?

Sweet Breeze Resort (Book 6): Can Gina manage her business across the sea and finish the remodel at Sweet Breeze, all while developing a meaningful relationship with Owen and his sons?

Rainforest Retreat (Book 7): As their paths continue to cross and Lawrence and Maizee spend more and more time together, will he find in her a retreat from all the family pressure? Can Maizee manage her relationship with her boss, or will she once again put her heart—and her job—on the line?

Getaway Bay Singles (Book 8): Can Katie bring him into her life, her daughter's life, and manage her business while he manages the app? Or will everything fall apart for a second time?

Books in the Stranded in Getaway Bay Romance series

The Perfect Storm (Book 1): A freak storm has her sliding down the mountain...right into the arms of her ex. As Eden and Holden spend time out in the wilds of Hawaii trying to survive, their old flame is rekindled. But with secrets and old feelings in the way, will Holden be able to take all the broken pieces of his life and put them back together in a way that makes sense? Or will he lose his heart and the reputation of his company because of a single landslide?

The Overboard Mistake (Book 2): Friends who ditch her. A pod of killer whales. A limping cruise ship. All reasons Iris finds herself stranded on an deserted island with the handsome Navy SEAL...

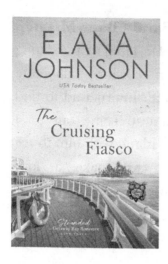

The Cruising Fiasco (Book 3): He can throw a precision pass, but he's dead in the water in matters of the heart...

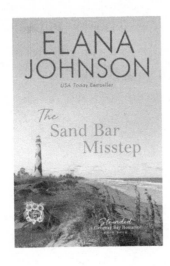

The Sand Bar Misstep (Book 4): Tired of the dating scene, a cowboy billionaire puts up an Internet ad to find a woman to come out to a deserted island with him to see if they can make a love connection...

About Elana

Elana Johnson is the USA Today bestselling and Kindle All-Star author of dozens of clean and wholesome contemporary romance novels. She lives in Utah, where she mothers two fur babies, works with her husband full-time, and eats a lot of veggies while writing. Find her on her website at feelgoodfictionbooks.com

Made in the USA
Monee, IL
21 July 2024

62412955R00152